Mollie's body was practically tied in knots and her left arm was asleep and throbbing along with the scratches she'd gotten that afternoon. Soon, not only did everything hurt, everything itched too and there was no way she could maneuver to scratch any part of her body. Maybe she'd fallen into a patch of poison ivy. It wouldn't surprise her. Tomorrow she'd probably be covered with ugly red splotches.

She tried to concentrate on what was going on outside her sleeping bag instead of inside. She could hear Winston barking and a loud rustling sound nearby. Then she heard some branches snap underfoot. It would take something very big to snap so many twigs with a single footstep. And that something very big was coming very close to her. Something tugged at the corner of her sleeping bag. *Oh, no,* Mollie thought, *it really is the bear!*

FAWCETT GIRLS ONLY BOOKS

SISTERS

SISTERS
OUT OF
THE WOODS

Jennifer Cole

FAWCETT GIRLS ONLY • NEW YORK

RLI: VL: Grades 5 + up
IL: Grades 6 + up

A Fawcett Girls Only Book
Published by Ballantine Books
Copyright © 1987 by Cloverdale Press, Inc.

Library of Congress Catalog Card Number: 86-91393

ISBN 0-449-13210-2

Manufactured in the United States of America

First Edition: April 1987

Chapter 1

*M*ollie Lewis put her hands on her hips and assessed the large stack of clothes on her bed. It wasn't easy to select just the right things for a weekend camping trip, but she felt satisfied that she'd done a good job.

At fourteen, Mollie knew how important it was to have the right clothes for the right occasion and how important it was to look one's best, whether at home, at school, or on a hike. She always tried to make the most of her thick blond curls and big blue eyes—and downplay her curves, which, she was convinced, were often unnecessarily pronounced. Right now, she was pretty sure she'd packed everything she could possibly want or need for three days in the woods and she felt proud.

She looked up at the sound of a knock on her door. "Come in," she called out as her older sister, Cindy, appeared. In contrast to Mollie, Cindy looked like the quintessential California Girl. She was slender, with a natural athlete's body, sun-bleached blond hair and sparkling green eyes. Her skin was perpetually tan—except for her nose which was perpetually sunburned and peeling.

"You moving out, Shrimp?" Cindy asked, glancing at the mound of clothes on the bed.

"Very funny, Cin. I'm packing for the weekend," Mollie said impatiently.

"All *that*?"

"Sure, what's the matter with it?" Mollie challenged her sister.

"Well, for one thing, Alta Via State Park is a little short on porters ..."

"I can carry this stuff myself. It'll all fit in my backpack."

"Uh-huh," Cindy said without conviction. "What are you taking? Give me a guided tour."

"Sure," Mollie agreed. "I read this article in *Seventeen* about packing properly for a trip and it said that if you weren't sure you'd have laundry facilities, it was absolutely crucial to have enough clothes. So, I'm bringing my primary outfits, plus backup outfits for all three days. And—"

"What are you doing with this embroidered top?" Cindy interrupted, picking up the delicate blouse from the top of Mollie's pile. "Is it primary or backup?" Mollie was so engrossed in the task she had set for herself that she didn't even notice the teasing in her sister's voice.

"It goes with my black linen pants," Mollie answered sincerely.

"Isn't that a little dressy for the mountainside?"

"Well, I guess it might be, but Sarah heard that Paul Markham and his family might be going to Alta Via this weekend. I thought I ought to have *some*thing kind of fancy, you know? Paul's in your class. You must know him. He's the funniest, most gorgeous guy in the junior class, maybe even the whole school."

"Yeah, this week," Cindy said, rolling her eyes toward the ceiling. She couldn't believe how much time Mollie spent thinking about boys and how she managed to arrange everything in her life to catch them. Sixteen-year-old Cindy was much more interested in sports and outdoor activities, especially surfing. She'd had boys as friends all her life and they just didn't seem that special to her, except for one, of course. She'd been going out with Grant MacPhearson, a star surfer from Hawaii, for several months now. Cindy laughed loudly as she tried to imagine herself wearing linen pants on a camping trip. It was too much. What would Mollie think of next?

"Stop laughing at me!"

"It's not you, Shrimp. It's just something that popped into my head," Cindy said, trying to stifle her laughter behind her hand. "You should be reading *Field and Stream* before going on a camping trip, not *Seventeen*. You've got way too many clothes here, and they're all too dressy for the woods. Besides, you haven't even included your hiking boots yet."

Mollie looked at the pile of clothes once again and realized Cindy was right. She *had* forgotten her hiking boots. She was certain she would have remembered them sooner or later without Cindy reminding her, but it was typical, she thought, that her sister would butt in, thinking she had the answer to everything.

"Here, I'll help you put some of this stuff back," Cindy offered.

"No, that's okay," Mollie told her. "I'll do it myself." She had no intention of putting anything back and she didn't want Cindy clucking her tongue like a mother hen while she figured out how to get her clothes into her backpack.

"Okay, see you downstairs," Cindy said, shrugging. "Dinner's going to be ready in ten minutes."

"Okay," Mollie said.

On her way downstairs, Cindy heard the phone ring. She raced the rest of the way down to answer it, but before she got there, her mother picked it up.

"Howdy!" Cindy said as she entered the kitchen. Her older sister, Nicole, was standing over the stove stirring a pot of something that smelled delicious.

Nicole turned slightly and greeted Cindy with a nod, pushing a strand of her silky brown hair off of her face with the back of her hand. "You're awfully friendly tonight," Cindy said sarcastically. "What's wrong?"

"Nothing," Nicole answered glumly.

"Well, I don't know what's the matter with you. Here we are the day before leaving on a great weekend camping trip and you're not excited. It's going to be fantastic—hiking, fishing, climbing, sleeping under the stars! Doesn't it sound great to you?"

"Ma chère sœur"—Nicole started to say. Cindy cringed. Seventeen-year-old Nicole was fascinated with everything French and frequently slipped into the language (her best subject at school, naturally). But Cindy knew whenever Nicole called her *ma chère sœur* (my dear sister) she was being sarcastic. Cindy really didn't want to hear what would come next but she braced herself for whatever Nicole had to say.

"—It may be that your idea of a fantastic weekend is hiking, fishing, and all the rest of that outdoors camping stuff, but *mine* is not. Particularly when it happens over the same weekend as the French Club's Film Festival."

"But you've seen all those movies dozens of times already, haven't you?"

"Of course I have, Cindy. But I learn something every time I watch one. I mean, that's like asking you why you'd want to play tennis again after you've already played it once."

Cindy didn't think they were at all the same thing, but she could see how Nicole could make that mistake. After all, anybody who could live in beautiful Santa Barbara, a town that offered opportunities to be involved in so many outdoor activities year round, and who chose to be fascinated with a language and culture more than six thousand miles away in France—well, a person like that could make all kinds of mistakes.

Nicole pulled a roasting pan out of the oven and lifted it to the trivet protecting the counter.

"I'm going to finish my last math problem, Cin. I'll be back in a few minutes. Set the table, huh?" With that, she swept out of the kitchen.

Cindy shook her head in amazement. She got out the placemats, utensils, and napkins and began positioning them at the table. It didn't surprise her that both of her sisters seemed to have confused notions about a camping weekend. She was very used to the three of them seeing things differently. Their father sometimes teased them about their differences. He said that if a baseball landed in their back yard, Mollie would wonder if a handsome boy had thrown it, Cindy would wonder if she could throw it back as far as it had come, and Nicole would say *"Comment dit on 'baseball' en français?"* They all laughed when Mr. Lewis said that, but Cindy suspected he was right.

The Lewises' shaggy Newfoundland, Winston, rambled into the kitchen and nuzzled Cindy, looking for affection.

Cindy patted his head tenderly and said, "So, how about you, Winston? Are *you* as excited as I am about the trip to Alta Via State Park? You know how to have a good time outdoors."

He responded with a whimper that had only one possible interpretation: hunger.

"You want some dinner, don't you?" she asked, bending down to pick up his dish. Just as she put the filled dish back on the floor a few seconds later, her parents came into the kitchen.

"What's for dinner?" her father asked.

"Something Nicole dreamed up, as usual. I hope the dream wasn't a nightmare!"

Cindy finished setting the table and poured the milk while her father brought out the serving bowls and her mother put the bread on the table. "Listen, I'm taking a poll," Cindy said. "I'm trying to find out what everybody wants to do first when we arrive at the campsite in Alta Via tomorrow afternoon. So far, Mollie wants to change into a drop-dead outfit and look for some junior boy. Nicole wants to learn the French names for different kinds of trees, and Winston wants to eat. How about you guys?"

"Sounds like situation normal," Mr. Lewis said with a laugh. "But, Cindy," he said, glancing at Mrs. Lewis, "I'm afraid we've got a problem—" The look on his face told Cindy it was bad news. "Listen, why don't you call your sisters down and we'll talk about it over dinner."

Within a few minutes, all five Lewises were at the dinner table. When everyone was served, Cindy said, "Okay, Dad, what's the bad news?"

"It's Gramma," Mrs. Lewis began. "She's had an accident and we think she needs our help."

"What happened?" Nicole asked.

"Well, you know your grandmother," Mr. Lewis went on. Indeed, they did. Gramma Lewis was one of their favorite relatives. She had an incredible supply of energy, surpassed only by her aspirations. "When she was out mowing her lawn yesterday, she came across a baby bird that had fallen out of its nest. Gramma immediately got out her ladder and carried the bird back up to its home in the big old maple next to her garage. So far, so good. On her way down, though, her foot slipped. She fell onto the garage roof and broke her arm. She spent the night in the hospital and could stay there another couple of days, but she hates it and wants to go home. She didn't even plan to let us know what happened, but she figured maybe if we talked to her doctor and promised to help her out at home, she could leave the hospital sooner. It's really nothing serious. She's just in a little pain right now."

"When do we leave for Gramma's?" Mollie asked. Her sisters nodded in agreement. A camping trip would be fun, but Gramma Lewis came first.

"Well, that's the thing," Mrs. Lewis said. "Gramma needs help, not houseguests. She says to tell you the baby bird is doing fine and so is she—and you three shouldn't worry about either of them. But your father and I have talked about it and we think the two of us should go to Gramma's over the weekend. You girls stayed together for ten days while we went to Japan and you managed very well when I was in the hospital last month having my appendix out. You can certainly hold down the fort for a three-day weekend."

Nicole thought about what her parents had said. It made complete sense. Except for one thing. Although she herself was lukewarm about the camping trip, she knew that her sisters were both very eager to go and three-day weekends don't come that often. She was afraid that the disappointment would be too much for them and they would be grumpy all weekend and take it out on her. Besides, being the oldest she felt she should take charge.

"Of course we can take care of ourselves. Don't give it a second thought," Nicole told her parents. Then she continued. "Actually, I have a great idea. Why don't the three of us go on the camping trip by ourselves while you're at Gramma's?"

Cindy couldn't believe her ears. "What about your French Film Festival?" she blurted out. She didn't want to be blamed for Nicole missing it.

Nicole blushed. "I made a mistake, Cin. The festival isn't until next weekend."

"And you're afraid we'd reschedule the camping trip for then?" Cindy asked.

"Well, I—" Nicole began to protest.

"No need to say another word, Nicole," Cindy assured her, exchanging glances with Mollie.

Mr. and Mrs. Lewis conferred briefly. Then Mr. Lewis spoke. "You know, Nicole, your mother and I talked about the possibility of the three of you going camping together without us, but we felt the decision would have to come from you. We've been to Alta Via several times together and you all must be pretty familiar with the area by now. If you girls want to go, that will be fine with us."

The girls could hardly believe it. Cindy let out a whoop and Mollie bounced up and down in her seat. What an opportunity!

"Boy, you guys are the greatest!" Mollie said.

"Well, I don't know," their father said with a sly smile. "You don't think we're asking too much of you—"

"No way!" Cindy countered. "All you're asking is that we have a great weekend."

"That's true," Mr. Lewis agreed. "But we're also asking you to all cooperate for three days. That's the most important part of camping."

"No problem, Dad," Cindy assured him. "It's the kind of setup where the three of us work best together. I mean we all balance each other out." She didn't feel as confident as she sounded, but apparently she sounded confident enough because her mother agreed.

"Just what your father and I were hoping you would say," Mrs. Lewis said. "Now, we've got lots of work to do before we all go off for our weekend trips. We're leaving for Gramma's at noon tomorrow so we'll be gone by the time you get home from school. You girls take the station wagon. I want you to leave by four in order to get to Alta Via before dark. Nicole and I have already planned all the meals, so the food's ready. Your Dad already stowed some of the camping gear in the car tonight, so all you'll really need to do tomorrow is load a few odds and ends and pack your own things."

"Don't worry, Mom. We can take care of ourselves," Nicole assured her.

"I know you can," Mrs. Lewis told her daughters. "It's whether or not you can take care of each other that concerns me."

Her command was met by three loud groans as the girls stood up and began clearing the table.

Chapter 2

$\mathcal{M}$ollie was the first one home from school the next day. Nicole had offered her a ride with some of her friends, but Mollie was feeling very grown-up, about to leave on her first weekend trip without her parents, and she wanted to be by herself.

Overflowing with excitement Mollie approached the house. She retrieved her key from her purse and unlocked the front door. She was nearly knocked down by Winston as he jumped on her in greeting. She returned his welcome with a quick hug, then glanced into the empty rooms on the first floor of the house.

Her parents must have left at noon, as planned, for Gramma Lewis's house. Mollie took the last diet soda from the refrigerator and went to her room. Dropping her book bag on her bed, she quickly changed into the new camping outfit she'd bought just for the weekend. Her new ensemble consisted of khaki shorts with big pockets and mid-thigh cuffs and a pale pink T-shirt topped with a khaki safari shirt with button-down pockets and straps across the shoulders. She straightened the collar, then turned to look at herself in the full-length mirror on the back of her door.

The outfit looked great, though she wondered if maybe she wasn't getting a little too heavy in the hips. She vowed to start a new diet right away.

Mollie took her soda and sat down at her vanity, admiring her reflection, and then pretended that the face which looked back her her was not her own but that of Paul Markham.

"Hi, Paul," she said sweetly. "Oh, you like my outfit? Thanks. It's nothing special. Well, sure, I guess I do have a flair for style ..." No need to tell him that Sarah had helped her put the outfit together. "But, you know, this is just for bumming around in the woods. I love camping out, don't you? Sure, we come here a lot."

Demurely, Mollie wedged her finger under the flip top of her soda and opened the can, waving off Paul's efforts to help her. Looking deeply into the eyes that met hers in the mirror, she lifted the can to her lips and drank. Soda dribbled onto her shirt.

"Darn," she said, wiping the dark brown liquid from her pink top.

Just then Mollie heard the front door open, *"Bonjour. C'est moi!"* Nicole was home.

"Hi, I'm up here. Cindy's not home yet," Mollie called out.

"Are you packed? I'm going to get the food together. You're in charge of the pets. Cindy can be in charge of camping equipment when she gets home. We leave in one hour exactly. Can you be ready by then?"

"Of course," Mollie said wearily, wishing as she often did that she was an only child. Sometimes Nicole had a touch of the drill sergeant in her. Mollie vowed that she'd never become that bossy, even when she was seventeen, and she particularly wouldn't boss anyone who was as old as fourteen and didn't need to be bossed around in the first place. She finished stuffing her clothes into her backpack. It took all her strength, and she made a mental note to unpack them as soon as they set up camp so they wouldn't wrinkle. She rolled her snacks and a couple of books into her sleeping bag along with her groundcover and toiletries.

She paused to go over in her mind exactly what she'd packed, making certain she hadn't forgotten anything. She had remembered her hiking boots *and* she had gotten her primary and backup outfits for each day into her pack. She hadn't needed Cindy to tell her what *not* to take any more than she had needed Nicole's lecture on what she *should* take while they were standing in the middle of the hall between classes at school. That had been totally embarrassing.

In spite of her sisters' misguided efforts to help her, Mollie was now satisfied that she had packed everything she could possibly need. While she fastened the Velcro straps of her pack, she imagined how the firelight would dance on her embroidered blouse, mesmerizing Paul Markham. Suddenly, she needed to talk to Sarah. She flopped down on her bed and picked up the phone. After all, she had an hour until it was time to go.

In the kitchen, Nicole was taking the last of the frozen foods from the freezer and carefully storing them in the ice chest. Not only would they stay fresh in the chest, but their coldness would keep other things, such as milk, soda, and fruit juice, cool as well.

"Hi, Nicole," Cindy greeted her cheerfully as she bounced through the door.

"Hi, Cin," Nicole returned. "Listen, I'm packing up the food. You're in charge of equipment. Mollie's in charge of pets. We're each responsible for our own clothes and stuff. We leave in an hour."

"Aye, aye, sir, I mean, ma'am," Cindy shot out. "Synchronize watches, uh—" she paused, looking at her bare wrist, as if waiting for a second hand to come to twelve. *"Now!"*

Nicole was not amused. "It's not easy to organize a trip like this. I have a lot of things to worry about."

"Well, you don't have to worry about the equipment. I did all the work last night with Dad. What I'm worried about is the food."

"Don't worry about the food. Worry about Mollie," Nicole said.

"Why Mollie?"

Nicole sighed. "Well, I saw her in school today, between French and Biology. I stopped to remind

her about things she ought to pack for the weekend and she ignored me completely."

"Maybe she didn't hear you," Cindy suggested.

"She was standing right next to me. And then
after school I was waiting for Bitsy to give me a
ride home and Mollie was leaving, too. I told her
she could ride with us, but she just walked off by
herself."

"When Mollie turns down a chance to ride in a
car instead of walking, something's definitely
wrong," Cindy said.

"You're not kidding," Nicole said. "I just hope
she remembers to pack some necessities and
doesn't have to borrow from us all weekend." She
paused for a moment and then said thoughtfully,
"You know what I think?"

"What?"

"I think that Mollie has suddenly gotten a bad
case of the Independents. I have a feeling she's
decided that older sisters are superfluous," Nicole told Cindy.

"Well, on the one hand, she might have a point,"
Cindy teased. "But on the other, she's way off
base."

"Get out of here!" Nicole said. "I've got to concentrate on our meals."

"You know, you might be right about Mollie,"
Cindy said, pausing. "Last night I was in her room,
and you wouldn't believe the pile of junk she was
planning to take on this trip. I told her what to
get rid of and what to include and she didn't even
thank me. I even offered to help her pick out what
to pack but she turned me down. At first I thought

she was just being ungrateful, but it could be that she just wanted to do it by herself."

"I think that's the answer. I just hope she doesn't do anything really foolish this weekend," Nicole said.

Cindy nodded in agreement and then left Nicole in the kitchen to finish organizing the food while she went to her room to finish her own packing. She shoved her toothbrush and Swiss army knife into her backpack, rolled up her sleeping bag with the groundcover, tied up the bundle, and took it out into the hall to carry downstairs. Outside Mollie's room, she paused, thinking she might go in and offer some assistance to her younger sister, such as making sure she didn't overpack. But she could hear Mollie on the phone.

Cindy didn't exactly eavesdrop, but she could hardly help hearing the conversation through the open door. Mollie's voice pealed out into the hall.

"Well, I know, Sarah," Mollie was saying. "Camping can be kind of fun and to tell you the truth, it'll be more exciting without Mom and Dad there. The only bad news is my sisters. We're talking bossy-city here. Mollie-do-this. Mollie-do-that. As if I didn't know as much about camping as they do, more than Nicole even. After all, I did go to camp for three years!"

Cindy gasped. Sure, Mollie had been to camp. She'd been to tennis camp for one year, Ballet camp for another year, briefly. And Mollie had also been to a kiddie day camp when she was a toddler. All of this hardly added up to experience in the great outdoors.

Mollie went on. "Anyway, if Paul Markham *is* at Alta Via, I'll make sure he finds me this weekend ... or, at least I'll find him. I'll bet you a twelve-inch pizza at Pete's, but it'll have to be one of the healthy ones with extras—you know, the California pizza with broccoli and spinach on it. I'm on a diet ..."

Cindy couldn't believe how dumb Mollie sounded sometimes. As if pizza with broccoli and spinach were on anybody's diet. But she knew it wouldn't do any good to tell Mollie and, besides, if she did, she'd have to let on that she'd heard the rest of the conversation. Resigned, she picked up her sleeping bag and backpack and darted downstairs to the kitchen where she reported the overheard conversation to Nicole.

"You shouldn't eavesdrop," Nicole reprimanded her.

"I was hardly eavesdropping. Mollie's door was open and she was talking at full volume. I'm surprised you couldn't hear her down here."

"Actually, I could hear part of it," Nicole confessed. "The part about Mollie-do-this, Mollie-do-that."

"So, what are we going to do?" Cindy asked. "She's going to be an incredible pain this weekend."

"There's nothing we can do," Nicole told her.

"Somebody's going to have to keep her in line."

"Come on, Cindy. Be fair. How quickly we forget. Don't you remember the time you entered the swim meet and didn't tell anybody?"

"Yeah. I remember. How about the time you signed up to be a model and didn't tell anybody?"

"Well, I think Mollie has just decided she's old enough to exist without the burden of a family— it's a feeling I remember well," Nicole confessed.

"Me, too," Cindy admitted.

Nicole nodded accordingly. "So, we do nothing. She'll learn better sooner or later."

"Or else we'll abandon her in the woods," Cindy joked.

"Hmmm," Nicole said as if considering the possibility. She closed the cover on the ice chest, and fastened it tightly. "Okay, Cindy, help me lug this to the car, will you?"

Cindy picked up one end of the chest. "It's Cindy-do-this. Cindy-do-that," she mimicked.

Nicole gave her a withering look. Laughing together, the two sisters stowed the food and the rest of the camping gear in the car. Then Cindy helped Nicole to finish packing her own things. By the time that was done, it was four o'clock.

"Come on, Mollie," Cindy hollered. "Time to leave."

"Okay, I'll be right there," Mollie called downstairs.

"Time to go, Sarah," she said into the phone. "Have a good weekend at the beach. I'll call you when we get back to report on Project Markham. Just don't forget the pizza you're going to have to buy me. Bye!" Mollie hung up and glanced at herself once more in the full-length mirror. Satisfied that she looked her best, she picked up her backpack and sleeping bag and carried them down the hall, nearly tripping on Winston who was sleeping on the stair landing.

"C'mon, boy," she invited him. Winston flapped his shaggy tail and stood up. "We're going camping, Winnie. You're coming, too. You've *got* to come," she told him. "After all, you're the only one on the trip who won't boss me. I get to boss you." Winston stood up and followed Mollie down the stairs. While she put her bags and her tent into the station wagon, Winston whisked past her, settling himself half on the tent, half on the ice chest. Mollie had the sinking feeling that bossing Winston wasn't going to give her the satisfaction she'd been hoping for.

"Ready?" Nicole asked.

"Ready," Mollie and Cindy answered together.

"Okay, all aboard!"

As Nicole got behind the wheel, Cindy slipped in beside her. Mollie was relegated to the back seat, as usual.

"Off we go!" Nicole announced. She backed the car out of the driveway and turned onto the street. Behind them, the garage door slid closed.

They were off.

Chapter 3

"Alouette, gentille alouette,
"Alouette, je te plumerai!"

*I*n the front seat of the car, Cindy and Nicole sang happily together. Mollie sat in the back seat scrunched up against the door trying to read an article in *Young Miss* about eye makeup. She regretted that she had packed only a minimum of her makeup for the trip, but, she realized, it really wouldn't make much sense to put on makeup when she couldn't count on the light being good and without easy access to running water to wash off mistakes. Still, she could study the makeup pointers now so she would be ready to use them on her first date with Paul Markham after the camping trip.

"Come on, Mollie," Nicole said. "You do a verse now."

"Verse?"

"Of '*Alouette*.' Didn't you learn it in French class last semester?" When Mollie didn't respond, Nicole went on speaking. "It's actually an appropriate song for a camping trip," she lectured. "Because the French Canadians—*Les Québecois*—sing it while they paddle canoes. It keeps the woodsmen paddling in time to the music and it controls their breathing rate. Isn't that wonderful?" she asked.

"French is your specialty, Nicole. If we learned it, I don't remember it. You guys go on singing as much as you like. I've got other things to do." Even to Mollie, the words sounded a little harsh as she said them, but she really didn't want to sing a dumb French song about plucking a nightingale. Besides, the singing wasn't making the miles go faster. In fact, they were hardly moving at all. From the traffic surrounding them, it seemed that half the residents of Santa Barbara were heading for Alta Via, too. They would be lucky if it weren't already dark by the time they got to their campsite.

Mollie put down *Young Miss* and picked up a sketch pad. She was taking an art class this semester and was trying to practice as much as possible. Her teacher had told the class to keep a sketch pad with them at all times. "You never know just when you'll need it most," she had said. Mollie was finding that she was right.

She'd seen an article in *Seventeen* last month that had a lot of neat hints in it about room decorating. She was currently working on a way to give her room personality. She had tried to redecorate a couple of times before and had always gotten sidetracked before she could finish. But that was a few years ago when she was always trying one new thing after another. She was pretty sure she could do it from start to finish now that she was older. The look she was trying to achieve was very modern and geometric—all lines and angles with basic colors on white.

Mollie sketched her "Room with Personality," first trying it with the bed against one wall, then another. She liked the second arrangement and began filling it in a bit. She added a new night table and a picture over her dresser. It was neat, but homey. She admired her sketch and then added a sleeping cat on the bed. She smiled at the effect. The Lewises had two cats, Smoky and Cinders, and they often curled up on Mollie's bed. She added a second cat to the picture.

Suddenly she got a sinking feeling deep in the pit of her stomach.

"Oh, no," she gasped.

"What's the matter?" Cindy asked, turning around to look at her sister and noticing the sketch pad. "Hey, that looks great. But didn't you forget to put in the piles of clothing that are usually scattered all over your room?"

When Mollie didn't laugh or get angry, Nicole glanced at her in the rearview mirror and said, "What's wrong, Mollie?"

"It's the cats," Mollie explained.

"You did a cute drawing of them," Cindy said.

"I'm not talking about the cats in my drawing," Mollie responded.

"Mollie," Nicole began, "what are you talking about? I'm getting a bad feeling about this. *Should* I be?" she asked.

"Uh, yeah," Mollie admitted.

"That's what I was afraid of," Nicole said.

"What did you do, Mollie?" Cindy asked, frowning. "Don't tell me you forgot to put out extra food for Cinders and Smokey for the weekend."

"Yeah, I did," Mollie confessed.

"Okay, Mollie," Nicole said wearily. "We'll stop at the next gas station and you can call the Robinsons. They've got a key to the house, and they can go over and leave out the extra food."

Even though it was the only way that was not super inconvenient (like going home again) to rectify the situation, Mollie hated the idea of calling the Robinsons. They'd been the Lewises' neighbors for years, but since Mollie was always the one sent into their yard to fetch things like baseballs or Frisbees, she was the one who got the looks of controlled annoyance. She didn't think the Robinsons liked her much. Well, she was the one who had goofed this time and the Robinsons were the only people who could bail her out.

"I sure hate to stop now," Nicole was saying. "We're getting pretty close. Maybe we could wait until we get to the campsite and then see if there's a phone there."

"We can't, really," Mollie said. "We have to stop, not at a gas station with a telephone, but at a supermarket with a telephone."

"We've got all the food we need," Nicole assured her.

"Well, I know *we* do, but good old Winston is going to need some food, too."

"You forgot to do *everything* you were responsible for?" Nicole accused, her voice rising incredulously.

There was no way to deny it. What she had done was bad, but somehow it seemed to Mollie that it was at least partially her sisters' fault. After all, they'd been in the house, chatting and helping each other. All their goofing around had distracted her and made her forget her job, she decided, conveniently forgetting that she'd spent almost a full hour on the phone with Sarah. "Yeah, I did forget, but don't forget that you two were chattering away in the kitchen so loudly that I couldn't think."

Mollie was so angry with what seemed to her to be her sisters' conspiracy that she couldn't go on. Her sisters were so outraged at her flimsy excuse, they could hardly speak to her. Nicole and Cindy exchanged knowing looks and then kept their mouths shut. After all, it was obvious what had happened, and yelling about it wasn't going to change the situation.

Half an hour later, they stopped at a convenience store with a telephone booth outside, and Mollie made the call. After a minute, she tromped out of the phone booth, looking more downcast than when she went in.

"What did she say?" Cindy asked, jumping out of the car to meet her.

"Mrs. Robinson was pretty grumpy about it," Mollie told her.

"Well, what did you expect?"

"I know, but I'm getting the feeling that everybody in the world except me thinks they're perfect and wants to hold it over me."

"Perfect!" Cindy repeated. "Perfect has nothing to do with it. What you did—or rather didn't do—was irresponsible. It was just one little chore. Nicole told you to put out extra cat food and pack food for Winston for the trip. It wasn't that much to ask, Mollie."

"Well, Nicole *did* tell me," Mollie said. "Nicole tells me everything. She doesn't ask. She doesn't discuss, she tells. She's such a boss. And you're no better."

Cindy was astonished that Mollie could find so many ways to embroider an excuse for not having opened two cans of cat food, but there it was. First, it was her and Nicole's fault for talking in the kitchen when Mollie required absolute silence to concentrate on her responsibilities, then it was Nicole's fault for *telling* Mollie what do to! Mollie wasn't making any sense at all. Cindy realized that Nicole was right. Mollie was having a bad case of the Independents and the only thing to do was to leave her alone, but it was tempting to try to teach her a lesson.

"I suppose you have a point," Cindy said, walking back to the car. But I don't know what it is, she said to herself.

Glumly, Mollie went into the little general store and bought enough dog food for Winston for the weekend. It wasn't the brand he liked, but it was all they had so it would have to do. When Mollie returned to the car, Nicole started the motor and they were off again, bumper to bumper all the way to Alta Via State Park.

After twenty miles of stony silence, Nicole broke the ice.

"How about a round of 'Row Your Boat' in three parts?" she said brightly.

"Make it two," Mollie said. "I'm not in the mood."

"Well I am," Cindy said. "I'll start." And she did. While her older sisters sang cheerfully, Mollie let her mind wander, going over her plans for the weekend. She had her pizza bet with Sarah, so she'd have to spend some time hunting for Paul Markham. That would be fun. She also wanted to do some sketching near the creek for an assignment for her art class. She had brought all her own equipment for camping so she wouldn't have to hang around too much with her sisters. She had her own snacks, lanterns, reading material, and tent. She had decided that if she was old enough to go camping without her parents she could do just as well without her sisters, too.

Mollie glanced up and realized the woods on the edge of the road looked familiar. They were actually getting near Alta Via. She remembered the big rock on the edge of the woods, and the graceful curve of the mountain beyond. Suddenly, she thought it looked almost too familiar. She noticed a small road leading off to the left and she was almost certain it was the entrance to the park.

"Hey, Nicole," she called out from the back seat. "You missed the turn."

"How could I have missed it? It's not for another five miles."

"Oh, yes it is," Mollie corrected her. "That was it back there."

Nicole glanced over her shoulder. Cindy looked as well. "I don't know," Nicole said. "I didn't see a sign."

"It sort of looks like it," Cindy agreed. "But I'm sure it's not for another five miles, too."

"Well, in just a minute, it'll be five miles *behind* us," Mollie told her sisters.

"Maybe you're right," Nicole said. "I'd better find a place to turn around."

While Nicole found a deserted gas station where she could make her turn, Mollie sat in the back seat, smug in the knowledge that she'd saved them a big detour. There was so much traffic that Nicole had to wait quite a while for an opening. And then, when she reached the turnoff Mollie had indicated, Mollie knew she'd been right to recognize it. It was the turnoff to the swimming hole they'd been to last summer. It was not, however, the turnoff to Alta Via State Park.

"Mollie," Nicole said, in a very controlled voice, as she maneuvered the car around to turn back onto the crowded road. "This weekend is barely begun and so far you are batting 'oh for two' as Cindy would say. Think you can straighten out your act?"

"Well, I'm sorry," Mollie said. She didn't sound a bit contrite. "I knew I recognized that road and if you and Cindy hadn't been singing that dumb song maybe my brain would have been working better. It's not my fault if I can't concentrate!"

Nicole and Cindy sighed. It was going to be a long weekend.

Chapter 4

*A*t last Nicole turned the car into the well-marked main entrance of Alta Via State Park and pulled into a parking space at the registration cabin. Mollie went in with her while Cindy remained in the car. While Nicole went through the check-in procedures, Mollie looked at the clipboard on the desk containing the weekend's registration list, her eyes searching for the name Markham. When she spotted it, she was so excited she let out a squeal of delight.

"Mosquito bite already?" Nicole asked suspiciously.

"Nope, I'm just glad to be here," Mollie assured her, glancing back at the list to get the campsite number. To her dismay, the park ranger had picked up the clipboard to make a note and she could no longer see it. She closed her eyes, wishing she had a photographic memory. She strained to recall the number next to the name. Was it 13? She thought so—unless it was 31. After all, she'd been reading upside down. Must be 31, Mollie assured herself.

"Okay, Mollie, here's the stuff," Nicole handed her the paperwork. "We're at site 15, which is a good one, right by the creek. You've got the map there," she said, pointing to the pile of papers she'd just given to Mollie, "You be my navigator."

"Okay, Nicole," Mollie agreed cheerfully, still floating with happiness over finding out where Paul's campsite was located—or at least knowing he was in the park. "And don't worry, this time I won't mess up, okay?"

"I hope not," Nicole said.

Despite the fact that Mollie didn't think her sisters were blameless in her goofs—they *had* been extremely bossy and had sung obnoxious songs in the car—she was still a little embarrassed about what she'd done. Or, in one case, not done. It was a little thing Nicole had asked her to do now—to direct her to the campsite—but she was determined to do it right. Besides that, if she studied the map, she'd know where to find site 31.

She sat in the backseat and held the park map up to the quickly fading sunlight coming through the window.

"Okay, take a right here," Mollie instructed. "There should be a sign to Koala Creek."

"There is," Nicole confirmed, swinging the car to the right.

"Then, the Commissary is on the left up here...."

"Check," Nicole said.

"Take the second right after that. Then bear to the left at the fork, and ..."

"... We're here!" Cindy announced.

"At last," Nicole said.

It was 6:30, at least an hour later than they had intended to arrive at the campsite. The sun was suspiciously near the mountaintops to the west. The girls knew that they really had a race on their hands to set up their tents and get their fire going before darkness set in. Pitching tents by moonlight was nobody's idea of fun, particularly if those clouds that hovered on the horizon moved in and dumped some rain on them.

They quickly unloaded the car, moving their food, tents, sleeping bags, clothes, and sporting equipment over near the circle of stones where the campfire would be. Mollie tied Winston to a pine tree. When everything was unloaded, Cindy and Nicole began to set up the big tent.

Mollie moved her smaller tent over to the other side of the fireplace and began to set it up herself. She was just about to drive the peg for the front guy line when she realized she'd placed the tent right over an old tree stump. Not a high one, just an inch or two off the ground. Just enough to really annoy anyone who was trying to sleep on top of it. She dismantled her little tent and looked around without success for a more suitable spot. The site had really only been prepared to hold the tent—the big one—and the place for it was smooth.

While Mollie struggled with her tent, her sisters were having their own problems with theirs.

Nicole tugged at one of the guy lines and the whole thing tilted toward her, threatening to collapse. She muttered something in French.

"What?" Cindy called from the other side.

"Oh, nothing."

"I thought I heard you say a French word that you definitely *didn't* learn in French class," Cindy said.

"You did," Nicole confessed. "This stupid thing has gotten the best of me."

"Well, it wouldn't if you didn't treat putting it up as a titanic struggle," Cindy said.

"But it *is* a titanic struggle," Nicole responded.

"It shouldn't be. I mean, it's like surfing. If it's easy, you're doing it right. If it's hard, you're doing it wrong."

"Cindy, that doesn't make any sense at all," Nicole snapped, tugging once again at the line. "I mean, this tent peg is supposed to be pounded firmly into the ground, like *this.*" Her emphasis coincided with an awkward blow with the mallet, driving the peg as much toward the ground as into it.

"Stop it, Nicole!" Cindy yelled. "You're messing it up and you're going to ruin the equipment so we won't have any place to sleep."

"Yeah, and it'll be all Mollie's fault!" Nicole said irritably.

There was a moment of silence while Cindy and Nicole regarded each other sternly. Then they burst into helpless laughter.

"Because she told you what to do?" Cindy asked with a smirk.

"No, because she's making so much noise on the other side of the campsite," Nicole said.

"Can you believe her?" Cindy asked.

"Yes, I believe her. I just wish I didn't have to be near her while she's going through this."

"It's really pretty silly," Cindy said. "But it's good for a laugh."

"A much deserved laugh," Nicole agreed, laying down the mallet. She sat down on the ground and Cindy quickly collapsed next to her.

"What would it be like if we behaved like that?" Nicole asked.

"Us?" Cindy said in a mock shock. "How could we possibly behave like that? We're perfect. At least I am."

"No, me. I'm the perfect one!"

"Are not!"

"Am too!"

But they couldn't go on. They burst into laughter again, giggling loudly—at Mollie expense—until the tears rolled down their cheeks.

On other other side of the campfire, Mollie finished driving in her final peg and surveyed her accomplishment with satisfaction. The tent was straight and it was on mostly smooth ground. She was proud of what she'd done.

She put a six-pack of diet soda into a string bag and walked down to the creek with it. Carefully, she tied the drawstring to a tree, allowing the cans to hang in the water where the icy stream could chill them. She returned to the campsite, picking some wild flowers on the way. She put the blossoms in a cup and set them in front of her tent. *Seventeen* couldn't have done it better.

She glanced across the campsite to see if her sisters had noticed. What she saw, however, was the two of them, sitting together, laughing helplessly at some private joke.

Well, she didn't need them. She went into her tent to lay out her sleeping bag and organize her things before dark. She decided she'd had enough of her sisters for a while. She was going to change into an appropriate outfit and see if she could find site 31. Paul would certainly be nicer to her than Cindy and Nicole. In fact, she decided, Attila the Hun would be nicer to her than her sisters were being.

Eventually, Cindy and Nicole got themselves under control and went back to work.

"You know, Nicole, setting up this tent might actually be easier as a one-person job than with you as helper," Cindy said.

"I was hoping you'd say something like that," Nicole said. "I'll start working on the fire."

"Great. What's for dinner? I'm so hungry, I could eat a horse."

"How about a dog?" Nicole asked.

"Winston?" Cindy asked.

"Not Winston," Nicole assured her. "Tonight zee dinnair is a famoos French deesh whoos name is *chien chaud*. You like?" she said with a phony French accent.

"Hot dogs?" Cindy translated. "I like."

"Zen I cooook!"

"Zen I set up zee tent wizout you to get in zee way."

"Zat's what I call teamwork!" Nicole said, heading for the ice chest. As she went, she thought about how it seemed that the further they got from home, the closer she became with her sisters—at least with Cindy. She wished Mollie weren't being such a pain.

Just then, Mollie emerged from her little tent. Nicole could barely believe what she saw. There Mollie stood in the middle of a state forest at a fairly primitive campsite wearing an embroidered blouse and some linen pants—an outfit Nicole happened to know Mollie had saved up six weeks of allowances to buy.

"What are you doing in those clothes?" Nicole demanded.

"Wearing them!" Mollie answered.

"Oh," was all Nicole could answer, and then she decided to try to reason with her little sister. "Mollie, you're going to tear them to pieces in these woods."

"Doing what?" Mollie asked.

"Well, gathering some kindling for me, for starters."

"How did that get to be my job?" Mollie asked, in a tone of voice that clearly conveyed the message that gathering kindling was a job well beneath her dignity.

"It's a job that needs to be done," Nicole said. "I'm getting ready to cook. Cindy's finishing with the tent. What needs to be done next is gathering kindling."

Mollie didn't know how to respond. Gathering sticks for kindling was a baby's job. It was a job she'd been assigned on a campout when she was four. Maybe if Nicole hadn't said what she did next, Mollie would have gone ahead and gotten the kindling, but Nicole did, and it made Mollie very angry.

"And please see if you can do *this* job without messing up," Nicole asked.

Furious, Mollie stomped off into the woods.

Chapter 5

*M*ollie had been in such a hurry to leave her campsite, she hadn't even bothered to find a trail. She just ran straight into the woods. When she did find a trail, she wasn't certain which trail it was, but she knew that if she kept on it for a bit, she'd find another campsite, and once she'd found another campsite, she would know how to find number 31, temporary home of the funniest and cutest boy in the junior class.

Or so she hoped.

Besides trying to boss her around and making fun of her with Cindy, another one of Nicole's offenses against Mollie had been taking charge of the map of the campsites after their arrival. But she thought she remembered the park layout.

Just then, her footpath crossed another trail. She supposed it really didn't make much difference which way she went. After all, when you don't know where you're going, no way is right, but then, no way is wrong, either. She turned left.

She was walking up a slight incline so she concluded she was probably walking away from the creek. That was good. Number 31 was near Pine Ridge. She recalled that from her earlier glimpse at the map. But then, with a sinking heart, Mollie realized that the notation "The Heights" on the map meant that it was high. That meant that it was up. That meant that she was going to have to climb. She hoped she wouldn't have to climb too much. And, looking at the darkening sky, she hoped she wouldn't have to climb too long. Night was not far off, and she didn't have a flashlight.

Mollie heard voices so she knew she was near a campsite. She couldn't see the number at the entrance so she thought if she could go around it, she could find out where she was without bothering the other campers. She circled clockwise, keeping the sounds of the voices to her right. But she was listening too hard and not looking hard enough.

Suddenly, her right toe got lodged under the branch of a fallen tree. Just when she thought her foot ought to be in one place, *it* thought it ought to be in another and the result was disaster. Desperate to balance herself, she grabbed for a branch with her left hand. Instead of stopping her fall, the branch bent under her weight. She grasped it tighter, then realized it was completely covered with thorns. She quickly let go and the last sound she heard before landing next to the fallen tree was the terrible ripping sound of her pants, which had also gotten caught by the brambles. The first sound she heard as she landed was the unmistakable squish of mud. She was the first person in history to find a swamp on a mountain, and then she had to fall into it.

Mollie's immediate instinct was to cry out, but she knew that if she did, that would summon whoever was at the campsite. She could just see somebody coming across her in this state and laughing at her. That would be bad enough from a stranger, but she could barely begin to think how she'd feel if it were Paul Markham. She sat still for a moment, trying to calm herself, then decided to see how bad it really was.

It was really bad.

First of all, her left hand was a mass of scratches where she'd held onto the thorny branch. They weren't deep or dangerous scratches, but they stung and there was just enough blood to stain her embroidered blouse, probably permanently. Besides, scratches just didn't look all that attractive. Next, she was awfully sore where she sat down and she figured she could count on a gigantic black and blue mark in due course. And, speaking of her backside, she found her black pants in shreds underneath all the mud. Totally irreparable. Then, Mollie couldn't help herself. She put her head in her hands and cried.

"Okay, the tent's all set up, Nicole. How are you coming with dinner?" Cindy asked, emerging from her final triumph of driving in the last peg.

"I'm coming along fine, but the fire's not," Nicole answered.

"What's the problem with the fire?"

"No kindling. Miss Know-it-All has disappeared into the woods, ostensibly in search of some kindling, but, judging by the glamorous outfit she chose, I suspect she's actually in search of some bigger prey and may not return for a while."

"Can you believe it?" Cindy planted her hands on her hips and shook her head.

"You should have seen what she was wearing," Nicole said.

"Not the black linen pants!"

Nicole nodded. "Topped with her embroidered blouse."

"I can't believe she actually packed that. If she does find Paul, he'll be laughing too hard to fall in love."

"Paul?" Nicole asked. "Who's that?"

"Paul Markham. He's a junior at Vista. I've seen him around, but I don't know him too well. Anyway, Sarah told Mollie he'd be here this weekend and apparently Mollie's developed a king-size crush on him."

"Isn't he the guy who used to work at Pete's Pizza?"

"Yeah. He was terrific about giving lots of extra cheese at no extra charge," Cindy said.

"Too bad he doesn't still work there. Then Mollie wouldn't have to chase him through the woods. She could just go pig out on pizza all day."

"Yeah, well, now I've heard he's working at the hardware store and Mollie can't very well develop a sudden interest in nuts and bolts, can she?" Cindy asked.

"I suppose she could sign up for Shop next semester," Nicole suggested.

"And wear an apron that doesn't match her nail polish? Not likely."

"I guess you're right," Nicole agreed. "Anyway, if Paul is supposed to be here this weekend, that may explain why Mollie was hanging over the ranger's shoulder at the registration desk trying to read something on his list. She got awfully excited while we were in there."

"I guess she must have learned where Paul's campsite is."

"Okay, now I understand and now we know where we can find Mollie. Let's go pick up some kindling and get a bucket of water. I'm hungry and I don't want to wait for Mollie to eat. After all, if she's so independent, she can live on nuts and berries, right?"

"Or love," Cindy agreed, picking up the jug and following Nicole to the stream. "Actually, Nicole, you might be on to something."

"On to something?" Nicole asked, putting twigs into the paper bag she was carrying.

"It just occurred to me that we might have the perfect opportunity to teach Mollie something...."

"You're not talking about some kind of practical joke, are you?" Nicole asked.

"*Me?* A practical joke? Whatever would make you think that?"

"Well, I was just remembering the time you watered your math teacher's plants with green ink."

"They never looked better," Cindy assured her.

"Yeah, and I never knew you to watch the telephone so carefully—just in case Mrs. Bricken figured out who had done it and decided to call Mom and Dad."

Cindy dunked the jug into the stream and waited while it filled with cold water. "You know," she said thoughtfully, "that wasn't as scary as the time I took the jar of moths to the movie house."

"But you freed the evidence," Nicole said.

"Sure, but I still had the jar. I put it in my pocket before we left the theater. I was sure they'd search me and find it and when they didn't, I was still sure the police would be combing the garbage dump for a jar with traces of moths inside and nail me with fingerprints."

"Ah, that's what made you decide to forego a life of crime?" Nicole asked.

"No, it's what made me decide to wear gloves the next time I try it." The jug was full. Cindy stood up and turned back toward the campsite, barely noticing the canoe approaching from upstream.

"So what's the idea you have, Cindy?" Nicole asked.

"Well, I was thinking that this might be a good time to see how independent the shrimp really is."

"You want to abandon her in the woods the way you suggested before we left home?"

"No, but I think that we can take advantage of the opportunity to set something up while she's off in search of Paul Markham."

Just then, the canoe bumped unceremoniously into the shoreline.

"Did I hear my name?" a voice asked.

Mollie stood up uneasily. The scratches on her hand stung even more now and the bruise on her backside throbbed, but she knew it was getting too dark to continue to sit alone in the woods. She needed to get back to her campsite and at this point, the last person in the world she wanted to see was Paul Markham.

She decided that her original course was best. She would continue around the campsite that was nearest, figure out from its number just where she was and find her way back to campsite 15 from there. Carefully, she approached the voices.

But as soon as she stepped into the clearing, she was sorry. For there, staring at her, were no less than twenty girls, all between ten and twelve years old and all in uniform.

"Hey, look at the poor lady!" one said, pointing at her.

"That's no lady, that's a girl!" said another. Mollie didn't think that was a compliment, but she didn't care.

"Can you help me?" Mollie asked.

"Maybe," one of the girls said warily. "What do you want?"

"I just want to know where I am," Mollie confessed.

"That's easy," one of them retorted. "You're lost!"

They all giggled.

Mollie didn't. She wondered where the scouts' leaders were. Maybe they'd escaped, she thought. Lucky them.

"Hey, you're wounded!" a redheaded girl cried out.

"No kidding," Mollie said dryly. "Look, I just want to get back to my campsite. If you'll tell me what campsite I'm at, and lend me your site map, I'll leave you to your fun."

"First Aid!" the redhead called.

"I'll get the kit," another assured her.

"But I get to put the gunk on. I didn't get that badge yet, so it's my turn."

"I don't need any gunk," Mollie tried to assure them. "I just want to get back to my own campsite."

"Think she might have a concussion?" one girl asked another.

"I don't know. What's the first symptom? I forget," her scoutmate answered.

"Throwing up! That's it," the first girl answered brightly. "Did you throw up?"

"No, I didn't throw up," Mollie said. "I don't have anything in my stomach to throw up. I'm hungry and I want to get back to my campsite. Please tell me where I am."

"Food! She needs food!"

"I'll give her some of my slumgullion. I don't have my cooking badge yet."

"Slumgullion? What's that?" Mollie asked.

"Oooh! It's delicious. I'll get you some!" one of the scouts said dashing off to the campfire.

Mollie was completely powerless to stop the

girls from trying to help her with absolutely everything except what she really wanted.

"How come every time one of you decides I need something, the one who hasn't got a badge in it is the one who wants to help me?" Mollie asked.

"Because that's how we earn our badges," one of the girls explained.

Then, the First Aid kit and the badgeless scout appeared at Mollie's side.

"Let me have your left hand," the girl insisted.

Mollie relented, offering her limb for the cause of a badge. Then, while the gunk was being applied carefully, the scouts noticed Mollie had another pressing need.

"Oooh! Your pants!" one of them chimed.

"Go ahead and laugh," Mollie challenged her.

"Oh, no, but they're a mess," the scout told her.

"I noticed. Say, does one of you need a sewing badge?"

Three hands shot up.

Mollie was draped in a beach towel and given a bowl of slumgullion to eat while three girls tried to patch her pants. Slumgullion turned out to be a campfire stew. It had meat, potatoes, carrots, and something green—maybe spinach—in it. While she ate, she watched the girls try to figure out how to patch her pants. Since they were already a total loss, the girls certainly couldn't do any more harm to them and they might be able to at least mend them enough to cover her while she found her way back to the campsite. She really didn't want to walk back in her underwear.

Finally, Mollie saw the funny side of her predicament and laughed while she chewed on some unidentifiable piece of meat from the slumgullion.

When she was fed, bandaged, and patched, she asked her original question again. Only this time she phrased it differently.

"Anybody here need a land navigation badge?"

Four hands shot up.

"Let's go," Mollie said.

Chapter 6

"*H*ave you finished yet, Nicole?" Cindy hissed. "I think I hear her coming." She didn't want Mollie to catch them inside her tent.

"Almost done," Nicole answered from inside Mollie's tent. "Hold her off a bit."

"Easier said than—oh hi, Mollie," Cindy said, turning to her younger sister. "Are you okay, we were—my goodness! What happened to you?" she asked, noticing the bandages on Mollie's hand underneath the bundle of small sticks she was carrying.

"Oh, it's nothing," Mollie answered, as casually as she could, limping toward her tent.

"Your pants!" Cindy exclaimed. "They're ruined!"

Mollie turned. "You don't like the sewing job?" she asked.

"Well, it's interesting, to say the least," Cindy told her. "You did it with natural fibers?"

"Uh, sort of." Mollie's scouts hadn't been able to find a needle and thread, so they had sewn a patch on her pants with leather thongs through holes punched with an awl. It was probably not a look Parisian designers would want to copy right away, but it did cover up her underwear. Mollie didn't much want to talk about her clothes. She knew her hand would be fine, but the linen pants and bloodstained blouse had cost her a bundle.

"If you don't mind, Cindy, I think I'll just slip into something more comfortable. In fact—"

"Hi, Mollie," Nicole approached and joined the conversation from behind Cindy.

"Hello, Nicole. Here's your kindling," Mollie said, handing her a bundle of sticks the scouts had collected for her.

"Thanks, but we already had dinner. Have you eaten?"

"Yes, I have," Mollie said. She rolled her eyes heavenward.

"Say, did you ever find Paul Markham?" Cindy asked her.

"Where do you think I've been?" Mollie asked, hoping her sisters would think he'd been the one to help her out and to feed her the dinner she'd eaten. "I think I'd better change my clothes now."

"Okay, Mollie. We'll see you by the campfire. S'mores in five minutes flat!"

"I'll be there," Mollie said, climbing into her tent.

Mollie took one step inside her tent and her jaw dropped in horror. Her clothes, her sleeping bag and all of her things were scattered all over the place. Her backpack had been turned inside out.

"Hey, who did this!" she yelled.

"Did what?" Nicole called back across the camp-fire. She and Cindy exchanged looks.

"Who made the mess in my tent?"

"What mess?" Cindy asked innocently.

Mollie emerged from her tent holding a tangle of clothes in one hand and shredded papers in another. Her face was flushed with anger.

"Who did this?" she demanded.

"Oh, no!" Cindy exclaimed in horror. "What on earth do you think happened?"

"Oh, how awful!" Nicole piped in. She hadn't gotten a part in the school play, but she knew how to act on cue.

Mollie glared at her two sisters. "You did this, didn't you?" she accused.

"No way!" Cindy said.

"How could you think such a thing?" Nicole asked.

Mollie didn't think for a minute that her sisters hadn't pulled the prank, but she decided to give them the slight benefit of the doubt and test them. "Well, if you didn't do it, then you'll certainly help me clean it up, won't you?" she asked.

"Of course we will," Cindy said.

"Absolutely!" Nicole agreed.

"You *will*?" Mollie asked.

They both nodded and came over to help their sister. Clucking their tongues at the terrible mess, they helped her straighten everything out and had the place shipshape in a few minutes.

"I wonder what really happened?" Mollie asked when they were done.

"I can't imagine," Nicole said. "But, you know, Cindy and I left the campsite to gather kindling before supper and for about fifteen minutes after to wash our dishes. Winston was barking like crazy while we were gone. Whatever happened must have happened then, don't you think, Cindy?"

"It must have, but really, the creek's not that far away. You'd think we would have seen who-ever—or whatever ..." Her voice trailed off in thought.

"Well, anyway, everything's back to normal now," Mollie announced, admiring her newly ordered tent. "I put some sodas in the creek to cool right after we arrived. They ought to be ready for drinking now. Either of you want one?"

"Oh, no thanks," Nicole told her. "I'm still stuffed from dinner and I want to leave room for S'mores."

"Yeah, it's too bad you weren't here. Nicole's *chiens chauds* were delicious. Are you sure you had enough dinner?"

"Yes, I'm sure," Mollie said. She was just as glad she didn't have to share her sodas with Cindy and Nicole. Although they had helped her with the mess, they seemed just a bit too matter-of-fact about it. Some doubt remained in Mollie's mind. Once she'd changed back into her safari outfit—which had gotten smeared with dirt during the mess-up in her tent, she walked down to the creek to fetch her sodas.

They weren't there.

The drawstring that had anchored the sack was

there. Some shreds of the sack were there. But the sodas were completely gone.

The doubt came welling up in Mollie's mind again and again she was certain her sisters were pulling some kind of practical joke on her. As she stomped back to the campsite, she decided she would not give Nicole and Cindy the satisfaction of her anger. She wouldn't even say a word about it. Anyway, she had some blueberries stashed in her sleeping bag for a late night snack—much better for her waistline than S'mores—so she'd have those instead.

Carefully, she controlled her anger as she re-entered the campsite.

"Get your soda?" Cindy asked.

"Nah, I changed my mind," Mollie lied, slipping back into her tent.

She turned her sleeping bag over and unzipped it, reaching for the bag of blueberries. The plastic bag was there, but it was ripped to shreds and the mashed remains of two or three blueberries stained it, as well as the inside of Mollie's sleeping bag.

That did it.

Mollie stormed back over to her sisters' tent and threw aside the covering cloth.

"I can't believe you two would sink so low," she began. Her face was flushed with anger. "You have ganged up on me to make this weekend absolutely terrible. Mom and Dad would never let you get away with this. First you rip my stuff apart, then you steal my sodas and now—"

"What are you talking about?" Nicole asked,

surprised, interrupting Mollie before she could mention the blueberries.

"Don't play Miss Innocent with me! I know what you two have been up to!"

Cindy and Nicole exchanged looks, shrugging their shoulders. They had been wondering why Mollie hadn't gotten angry right after coming back from the creek and discovering the soda cans were gone. Even though it seemed odd that Mollie should explode now, it didn't really matter. In general, things were going according to their plan. Then Cindy spoke. "You know what this might be, Mollie?"

"Yeah, I know. It's my two older sisters behaving like babies just because they don't want to go get kindling by themselves!"

"No, that's not right at all, Mollie." Nicole spoke in her no-nonsense older-sister-knows-best voice. It was a tone Mollie usually trusted. "Cindy and I had nothing to do with the mess in your tent or the missing sodas."

"You know," Cindy said. "Come to think of it, *our* tent was a bit messy when we got back from the wash-up. I thought *you'd* done it, but I didn't say anything—"

"—And I thought you'd done it," Nicole interrupted.

"Then who—or what—did it?" Cindy asked rhetorically.

"Hmmm," Nicole said. "It must have something to do with the ranger." Cindy nodded in agreement.

"Are you trying to tell me that a forest ranger

messed up our tents and drank my soda?" Mollie asked, astonished.

"No," Cindy explained. "A forest ranger came by when we were eating dinner and warned us that there had been some trouble in the park."

"Like fraternity boys, or something?" Mollie asked eagerly.

"No. Like bears," Cindy said.

"Give me a break," Mollie moaned.

"No, really," Nicole assured her.

"He was really cute, too," Cindy said.

"The bear?" Mollie asked.

"No, silly. The forest ranger. He had short brown curly hair and clear blue eyes. Oh, and every time he smiled, you could see those gorgeous dimples. Mollie, they would have made you melt." Cindy had stolen the description straight out of one of the romances Mollie loved to read.

"What kind of bear?" Mollie asked.

Cindy and Nicole spoke at once. "Brown," Cindy said. "Black," Nicole said. Then each corrected herself. "Black," Cindy said. "Brown," Nicole said.

"What we mean is that there were really probably two bears around—one black, one brown—at least that's what the ranger said," Cindy explained, giving Nicole a withering look. "The bear must have been here while we were at the creek. Remember how Winston was barking up a storm and we figured it was a raccoon or something? I guess it was *something*."

"Poor old Winston," Nicole added. "Boy, he must have been scared." Nicole sounded so sincere that Cindy was almost ready to feel sorry for Winston.

For a moment, Mollie was lost in thought. She had heard that, from time to time, bears would scavenge through human campsites at wilderness parks. They might do something like mess up a tent just to get at blueberries. Soda cans in a stream seemed a little farfetched, but then maybe the shiny aluminum cans would attract a marauding bear—black or brown. Mollie wondered if they were all in danger. Then, she wondered what the truth really was.

She stared into the flames of the campfire, hoping to find the answer in the yellow light that danced on the trees surrounding the campsite. She did. For there, carved into the bark of a pine tree, were five long, deep, parallel scratches that looked very much like the claw marks of a bear.

Chapter 7

"*O*h my God!" *Mollie said, staring at the claw* marks. Her sisters looked with her. "I wonder if there are any more." She stood up and ran over to the pine tree. On the opposite side she found a matching set. It gave her the shivers.

"Look! Over here!" Cindy yelled, drawing Mollie over to another tree. On it were an identical set of claw marks.

"No doubt about it," Mollie told her sisters. "It's a bear and it's a big one."

"Maybe we'd better pack up and go home," Nicole suggested.

"At this hour of the night? Don't be silly," Mollie said with authority.

"So what do you suggest?" Nicole challenged her.

"I'll tell you what I suggest. I read this book once, about pioneers and trackers and this is what they would do when they thought they were going to be attacked by a bear—"

"They'd climb a tree," Cindy said.

"Not at all. Bears can climb trees. I mean, look at those claw marks." She gestured at the scarred trees. "No, the thing to do is to get someplace where the bear can't reach you."

"In the car?" Nicole asked hopefully.

"No, Nicole. What you do is to make a sort of hammock."

"I thought you said the bears could climb trees," Cindy said.

"They can climb *big* trees, like the ones where they've made scratches. But they can't climb little trees, like saplings. So you sling your hammock between two saplings."

"What happens if the bear tries to climb the saplings?" Nicole asked.

"Bears don't climb saplings and that's that. I'm sure I saw something about it on a nature special on television once," Mollie told her sisters.

"Isn't that the show you were watching the night you and Sarah burned the popcorn and spent the whole time in the kitchen?" Cindy asked.

"Maybe," Mollie told her. "I don't remember. But no matter what, I'm sure the hammock thing is a good idea."

"Okay, well, it sounds good to me—for you to do, Mollie. But I think I'll stay in the tent," Cindy said. It was all she could do to keep from laughing.

"Me, too," Nicole agreed.

"And if Winston starts barking the way he did

before, we'll both jump into your hammock with you," Cindy told Mollie.

"As if I'd let you in," Mollie mumbled, heading for her tent.

Nicole and Cindy exchanged glances and winks and retired to the campfire for the evening. In a way, it was almost unfair to Mollie to take advantage of her inclination for the dramatic by telling her there was a bear in the woods. They'd had a laugh before her return about how vulnerable she was. Still, Mollie seemed badly in need of a lesson and Nicole and Cindy were seeing to it that she got it.

"Here, hand me a marshmallow," Cindy said.

"Mais, certainement," Nicole assented.

While Nicole and Cindy watched, Mollie struggled with the laundry rope they'd brought along for Winston. Carefully, she constructed a sort of cat's cradle between the two saplings about four feet off the ground. Next she laid her sleeping bag on the mesh and attached the corners very carefully so the bag wouldn't slip off. Then she tested the hammock's strength by leaning on it. It seemed satisfactory to her.

In fact, it seemed more than satisfactory. Mollie was so pleased with the results that she decided to test it out almost immediately. She glanced at her watch. It was 8:30—really still too early to go to bed (unless you happened to be a baby, like the kind of camper who would gather the kindling). So, she decided to perfect the sleeping hammock.

Mollie went back into her tent and emerged a few seconds later with her flashlight. With some more of the rope and some ingenuity, she devised a sling for the flashlight, which, if the wind didn't switch its position, would cause the beam of the flashlight to shine right on the pages of Mollie's magazine while she lounged in her hammock.

Next Mollie borrowed an aluminum foil baking tray from Nicole. She punched holes in the corners and threaded the last yards of rope through them. This, too, was suspended from the sapling's branches, almost level with the sleeping bag. It looked a lot like a bedside table.

"Pretty neat," Cindy said.

"Jealous?"

"Not really. I was just admiring your work. You really know a lot of stuff we've never given you credit for."

"Yeah, I know," Mollie told her. She was beginning to feel like Robinson Crusoe. She really felt badly that her sisters weren't taking the same precautions she was. She was worried about them.

"Won't you guys do anything to protect yourselves?" she asked.

"Nah," Cindy told her. "It's not necessary for us to do that. You see, the last time the bear came around, he went into *your* tent. It's your tent he'll return to, looking for whatever he was seeking in the first place."

"You sure?"

"Oh, absolutely. It's something that handsome ranger mentioned to us, too. Once a bear's attacked one tent, he'll return to that same spot."

Mollie was glad she'd made a protective hammock.

"I think it's time for a tryout now," she announced, appearing from her tent with a copy of *Seventeen*. "I'll take one of those cans of fruit juice for a snack, too."

"Sure thing," Nicole said, handing one to Mollie.

"Here, give me a hand up," Mollie asked.

Nicole made a stirrup for Mollie to step into. She placed one foot on it and hauled herself up onto the hammock. As quickly as she got up on one side, she came down on the other, landing unceremoniously on her bruised backside.

"Oooooow!"

"Looks like you need some stabilization," Cindy suggested.

"That's not all I need," Mollie complained, rubbing her bruise.

"Come on, Mollie," Cindy encouraged her. "I think the hard part is getting in. Once you're in, you'll be safe as can be."

"Sure," Mollie agreed. But she wasn't as certain as she had been five minutes before—or even thirty seconds before. Still, she was nowhere ready to admit defeat. "Okay, Nicole, you hold this side. Cindy, you hold the other."

Her sisters braced the hammock while Mollie climbed up into it and slid into the waiting sleeping bag. The last thing Nicole and Cindy saw, as Mollie's entire body, including arms, legs, and head, totally disappeared into the center of the sleeping bag, was her copy of *Seventeen*. Then after a moment it slid into the bag after her. Her weight had bent both of the saplings toward each other, turning Mollie's hammock into a V-shape. She was totally scrunched into a ball at the point of the V. One of her knees was pressed against one of her ears and she was slung only inches from the ground. It wasn't terribly comfortable, not at all what she'd had in mind.

"Want me to turn on the flashlight?" Cindy offered, snickering.

"Go away!" Mollie said. Mollie had the terrible feeling her Robinson Crusoe act wasn't working out the way she'd hoped. She knew she looked ridiculous. She didn't need to be reminded of that by her sisters.

In the sleeping bag, she knew she was perilously close to tipping over, either way, at any second. All dreams she had had of carefree sleeping were as far out of reach as her flashlight. If she made one move, any move at all, she'd go over and out, and she'd have to confess failure. In her sisters' eyes, Mollie figured her failure rate tonight was near 100%.

It had originally been Mollie's plan to test out her perfect hammock and then join Nicole and Cindy for S'mores before settling down to a relaxed night's sleep. That was a fine plan, except for one thing. She couldn't possibly get out of the sleeping bag. She did the only thing she could do under the circumstances.

"Good night," she called from her downy hiding place.

"Going to sleep already?" Cindy asked.

"Yeah, I'm really beat," Mollie said, hoping she

sounded sincere. "You know how it is—fresh air and all that . . ."

"Okay, then *bon soir*," Nicole said, stifling a giggle. *"A demain."*

"Same to you," Mollie said.

She closed her eyes.

Chapter 8

*N*icole and Cindy *retreated to their own tent* and stared at the precarious balance of their sister, her sleeping bag, and the none-too-secure V-shaped hammock. They had a feeling they wouldn't have to stare at it too long.

On the other side of the campfire, Mollie was suffering. Her legs were entwined with each other more than she thought they ought to be, but they were also scrunched up next to her body and surrounded by her arms. She was lying on her right arm and even after just a few minutes, it was clear her arm would be the first part of her to sleep, followed immediately by her left ankle. Why did her ankle hurt? Well, Mollie couldn't even begin to figure it out, but, as far as she was concerned, pain was pain and she was in it. That thought made her scratches start throbbing. Maybe they were becoming infected. Suddenly, not only did everything hurt, everything itched, too, and there was just no way she could maneuver to scratch any part of her body. Maybe she had fallen right into a patch of poison ivy and tomorrow she'd be covered with ugly red splotches.

Stop it, Mollie told herself. Concentrating on discomfort simply magnifies it. She knew that. She had to think about something else. She tried to clear her mind of all pain and discomfort but her thoughts kept returning to her trip into the woods. She thought she might die if her sisters found out what a fool she'd made of herself. Then she thought of how they probably already knew. The torn pants and her bandaged hand didn't exactly tell a story of triumph and glory.

Stop it, Mollie repeated to herself. Don't dwell on failures. Dwell on successes. That would be some trick today. Come to think of it, she couldn't come up with any. Well, she had set up this wonderful hammock of course, and she was enjoying the benefits of nature in this woodland wonderland. Yes, the benefits of nature, she thought. She decided to count them instead of sheep. Surely that would lull her to sleep even though she was absolutely, totally awake.

She listened carefully. She could hear her sisters talking, but there were other sounds, too. She could hear the shrill sounds of crickets chirping. *Chirrup chirrup.* They sounded very close. Then Mollie felt a tickle on her leg. She kicked and her hammock swayed wildly. Must be a cricket in the sleeping bag, chirping right near her ear. Swell, she thought. She decided to ignore it.

Next she heard the *ga-ronk ga-ronk* of a bull-frog. Then she heard the answering *ber-deep ber-deep* of a neighboring bullfrog—or was it a cowfrog, and had they just made a date? She decided it would be easier to try to sleep on a bed of nails by the side of a freeway than right where she was.

The leaves on the ground nearby rustled. Probably just a squirrel, Mollie thought. It got louder. Winston growled. Must be a raccoon. Winston barked. Winston *always* barked at raccoons.

But Winston also barked at bears.

Mollie listened very hard. The rustling continued, so did Winston's growling and barking. Usually, he wasn't much of a guard dog. He tended to jump up on strangers and welcome them into the Lewis home, but he was a little pickier about animals.

Mollie tried to picture what was going on outside by the sounds near the campfire, by the direction of Winston's barking, and by the loud rustling around. She heard some branches snap underfoot. It would take something very big to snap so many twigs with a single footstep. And that something very big was coming very close to her.

Next, she heard the animal prowling around her tent. She could hear the pages of a magazine rip. Winston continued to bark and growl. It sounded as if things were being thrown around inside her tent—just the way they had been before. Then the sounds stopped. There was silence for a few seconds.

The rustling began again and came closer to her hammock. Something tugged at one of her saplings. Her hammock bounced on the ground. Mollie realized that the creature, whatever it was— and by now, she was absolutely certain it was a bear—was tugging not at the tree, but at her failed bedside table. She realized that it was made of aluminum—nice shiny aluminum, just like the cans of soda, which she'd placed in the stream, that had attracted the bear.

Then, for the first time, it occurred to Mollie that she could scream. She could scream her head off and her older sisters would come running to her rescue. They would frighten the bear off with whatever it took—shouting and screaming, or wrestling the beast to death. Mollie decided to scream. But she couldn't. No matter how hard she tried, she couldn't get a single sound to come out of her constricted throat. She was simply too terrified.

The beast stopped tugging at her night table and began tugging at one of her saplings.

Bears can't climb saplings, she reminded herself. No bear in his right mind would climb a tree that couldn't hold his weight. Mollie was pretty sure she remembered that correctly, but then she realized that Cindy had been right. She and Sarah *had* spent most of the time during that television show coping with burnt popcorn and not studying the habits of bears. She quickly promised herself she would watch all the nature shows on TV—if only she could get out of this alive and whole.

Then she realized it didn't matter if bears could climb saplings or not. No bear would have to climb a sapling to attack her. She was only six inches above the ground. That was probably exactly the height of a bear's dining table, Mollie thought, miserably.

Finally, there was a tremendous jerk at one of the trees. It brought to an end the perilous balance of Mollie's hammock. The entire construction collapsed. Mollie, instead of being in a hammock that might dump her at any time, now found herself in a sack in which she was a helpless prisoner.

She found her voice at last. *"Help!"* she cried. "Cindy, Nicole, help me! The bear is attacking me! I'm stuck here. Come help me before I'm ripped to shreds! HELP!"

There was no answer to her cries. At first, Mollie thought her sisters must have fled, but then she realized that they never would have had a chance against the bear. It occurred to her that the bear might have eaten them first. But then why would he still be hungry? Her sisters were thin, but they were both tall—a lot taller than Mollie—so they should have been enough to fill him up.

Ugh! What a thought! But where were Cindy and Nicole? Mollie screamed again, hoping she could make enough noise to draw someone from another campsite before the fatal attack occurred.

Finally, she heard human noises, and relief rushed through her. She was sure her rescuers, whoever they were, could chase the bear away before it ate her. She waited for the melee to begin.

It didn't.

Instead, she realized through the haze of vanishing terror, the noise she was hearing was laughter—uncontrolled, smirking, snorting, giggling, human laughter.

"Get me out of here!" she demanded.

"As soon as we can, Mollie," Cindy's voice assured her.

"Why can't you do it *now*?" Mollie asked.

"Because we're laughing too hard," came a familiar male voice.

It was Paul Markham.

Chapter 9

"*I'm going to kill you*," Mollie promised, her voice muffled by the sleeping bag in which she was still trapped.

"Who are you going to kill?" Cindy asked.

"All of you."

"All four of us?" an unfamiliar male voice asked.

"Who's that?" Mollie asked.

"Mario," he said. "Mario Delavante." He was in Paul and Cindy's class. Mollie knew him vaguely because he hung out with Paul.

"Yeah, I'll kill you, too," Mollie promised.

"And the bear?" Cindy taunted.

"With my bare hands—"

"Then we won't let you out of there," Paul said.

"Let me out now!"

"Come on, Mol, you've got to promise first—" said Cindy.

"What do I have to promise?" Mollie asked.

"You've got to promise you'll laugh," Cindy said.

"Laugh! What is there to laugh at?" Mollie snapped.

"The situation," Cindy suggested.

"I don't think it's very funny. I'm pretty sure you wouldn't find it funny either if you were hanging in a sack from two trees and you couldn't get out and you were scared to death that you were about to be eaten by a bear, but it wasn't a bear at all, it was some mean, horrible, awful, joke that your sisters dreamed up, convincing you that bears were in the woods just so you would make a fool of yourself and get yourself all tangled up in your sleeping bag, looking like an idiot ..." But then, Mollie couldn't go on. The full impact of the situation finally began to hit her and she started to giggle helplessly.

"You okay in there?" Nicole asked solicitously.

"I guess so," Mollie sputtered.

"I think she's laughing," Paul said.

"Are you?" Cindy asked.

"Of course I am," Mollie told her. "Have you ever seen anything sillier in your life? I mean, this is totally absurd, isn't it?"

"Yeah, it is."

"So, let me out," Mollie said.

"It's a deal," Paul said. He and Mario began the rescue operation. But it wasn't easy.

First, they had to untie all the knots Mollie had made constructing her hammock.

"You're pretty good at knots," Paul said, admiringly.

"I'll thank you not to make any more fun of me," she said.

"No, I mean it," he said. "I spent three years in the Boy Scouts. I never saw work like this."

"I took a macrame class," Mollie explained.

Paul laughed. "You kidding?" he asked.

"No. If you want me to, I'll make you a plant hanger sometime." Or a noose, she thought to herself.

"Can we sling it between two trees?" he teased.

"No more remarks," she said smartly. But secretly, she was pleased that Paul had admired her work.

"I'd forgotten about that class you took," Nicole said.

"I remember it," Cindy said. "You did that right before Christmas last year so you could make plant hangers for everybody for Christmas. I've still got mine."

"Yours wasn't a plant hanger," Mollie said. "I made you a macrame belt."

"Maybe that's why I couldn't get the plant to stay in it!" Cindy said.

"And now you've made yourself a macrame prison," Paul said. "Yeow!"

"What happened? Break a fingernail?" Mollie asked.

"Very funny. No, I pinched myself in your macrame spider web," Paul said, but she knew he did think it was funny.

Mollie realized, with a great feeling of relief, that there actually might be a way to salvage the situation from entire disaster: To keep on laughing. She was still pretty annoyed with her sisters, but it was clear that she was making headway with Paul—and at least she'd won her pizza bet with Sarah.

"Okay, here you go," Paul said, releasing the final knot and letting the sleeping bag down to the ground carefully. Mollie emerged.

"Ta-da!" she said. Her sisters, Paul, and Mario applauded. "Now, if only I could wake up," she remarked, rubbing her right arm.

"You seem pretty awake to me," Paul said. "In fact, you seem pretty bright-eyed and bushy-tailed for somebody who was within inches of being eaten by a bear just a few minutes ago."

"Most of me is awake," Mollie said. "But there are a few parts that went to sleep some time ago and are in danger of sleeping through the night, notably my right arm, and for some reason, my left ankle." She tried to stand, but stumbled. Paul reached for her elbow to steady her. His grip was sure and comforting.

"Thanks," Mollie said, flashing him her brightest smile.

"Well, Mollie," Cindy said, "That was some show you put on."

"Uh, correction, Cindy. I may have been the star, but I think the producer, director, and writer ought to take a bow."

Cindy took a small bow. She could hear just a bit of ice in her sister's voice and she knew that in spite of Mollie's apparent good humor, she and Nicole were far from forgiven. Mollie's exemplary behavior at that moment could only be explained with one word—two, actually—Paul Markham. Cindy decided Mollie had been through enough. She'd probably learned her lesson by now. It was time to be civil again.

"Come on over and sit down by the fire, Mollie. You've had quite a trauma. What can we do for you?"

"Any of those *chiens chauds* left?" Mollie asked. Among the pains she was suffering were ones of hunger. The scouts' slumgullion had been neither good nor filling.

"Combien," Nicole said.

"Deux, si'l te plait," Mollie responded.

"What is this, French class?" Mario asked.

Cindy and Mollie laughed. "No," Mollie explained. "But our chef prefers to speak French and if you order in French, it gets the job done faster."

"So, what did you order?" Paul asked.

"Two hot dogs," Mollie told him.

"Ah, the old continental cuisine favorite!"

"No, the old campfire staple," Nicole corrected him, returning to the fire with two hot dogs speared on a stick.

Within a few minutes, Mollie was eating a perfectly cooked hot dog and was really feeling better about everything. Well, almost everything. She was still annoyed with her sisters, but the happiness at having Paul next to her overcame her distaste for her sisters' presence. They'd see how much she needed them!

While she finished up her supper, her sisters and the boys finished laughing about the practical joke. Paul was particularly proud of the bear claw scratches he'd carved into the tree. Mollie tried to laugh along with them to show she was a good sport, but it was hard. Being the object of someone else's good humor really was no fun, so she ate the last bite of her hot dog and smiled with as much conviction as she could muster.

"Okay, now is it time for S'mores?" Cindy asked.

"No," Nicole said. "Let's wait a while and have them just before we go to sleep."

"And it's not time for that yet," Paul said.

"No way. The night is yet young!" Mario said, sounding as if he'd just thought up the phrase.

"So what do you do for an encore when you've just rescued a maiden from the clutches of a brown black bear who likes to mess up tents, ravage soda cans, and steal blueberries?" Mollie asked.

"Blueberries?" Cindy and Nicole asked in a single voice.

"Yeah, blueberries," Mollie said. "You guys stole the blueberries from my sleeping bag."

"We didn't steal any blueberries from your sleeping bag," Cindy said, genuinely confused.

"We really didn't, Mollie," Nicole added. "But you know what, it was a hard task messing up your tent after the state you left it in. We definitely didn't touch your sleeping bag. It was all scrunched and messed up exactly the way you found it in your pigpen of a tent."

"I didn't leave my tent a mess," Mollie protested, recalling all the work she had put into making it just right before she'd left the campsite. "It was spotlessly neat when I left it."

"No it wasn't—" Cindy argued.

"Yes it *was*."

"Then *who* made the mess?" Cindy challenged.

Mollie figured it really wasn't worth arguing any more. Her sisters were obviously not going to admit that they'd been responsible for taking her blueberries, too. Well, that was fine with her. She'd had enough of this bear joke.

"I think it's time to change the subject," Paul said much to Mollie's relief. Nobody disagreed with him. "I think it's time for a moonlight canoe ride along Koala Creek. We can go look for creaking koalas! Who wants to come?"

"I'll go along," Mollie said. She had always enjoyed canoeing, and the chance to combine an activity she liked with a boy she liked was irresistible.

"Mollie!" Nicole said.

"Don't worry, Big Sister," Paul said in a reassuring tone. "We will take care of Mollie and we will bring her back, unharmed, within an hour. Although, to tell you the truth, from what we've seen tonight, I think Little Sister here can actually take care of herself."

That was the nicest compliment Paul could have paid her at that time, and the only compliment she could recall receiving all day. It sort of made up for his calling her Little Sister, which she liked about as much as she suspected Nicole liked being called Big Sister. Still, it seemed that Paul liked her, and it would be nice to spend time with someone who appreciated her ability to take care of herself. Proudly, Mollie stood up and followed the boys to their canoe. Paul handed her a paddle, and she settled comfortably into the center of the boat.

Chapter 10

*M*ollie held her paddle securely in her hands, her bandaged left hand cupping the end, her right encircling the neck. She swung it easily through the air and cut into the water, propelling the canoe along the creek.

They veered to the right. Mollie paddled quickly to straighten them out. They swung sharply to the left. She shifted her hands and thrust the paddle deeply into the water to stabilize them.

"What's going on?" she asked.

"We're paddling our own canoe," Paul said.

"Better known as going around in circles!" Mario said, and the two of them laughed uproariously. Mollie didn't see what was so funny about it.

"Well, if you'd each pick a side—a different one—to paddle on, we'd have a chance of going in a straight line."

"Who needs to go in a straight line?" Paul asked, thunking his paddle inexpertly against the side of the canoe. "The creek just carries us along, no matter what we do."

Mollie hauled in her paddle and laid it across the gunwales. There was no point in trying to struggle against these two. Besides, they were right. The canoe floated gently downstream, no matter what they did. She leaned her back against one of the struts and stared up at the skies. The moon was streaked with clouds.

"It's a beautiful night," she remarked.

Paul looked up, too. "Sure is," he agreed. "But where are all the stars?"

"They're behind the clouds," Mollie told him.

"Nope," he announced. "They're all at home in Beverly Hills!"

Mario and Paul laughed together. Mollie continued to stare up at the sky. The canoe veered dangerously to the left. She leaned over to the right to keep them from capsizing.

"And where are the planets?" Paul asked, oblivious to Mollie's actions.

"I give up," Mario said.

"They're in the garden—where you planeted them!"

"Oh, moan and groan!" Mario said, acknowledging the bad joke. Mollie didn't actually think it needed to be acknowledged. Suddenly Paul's much-touted sense of humor didn't seem quite so appealing to Mollie, but it sure appealed to Mario.

"And what about the sun?" Paul asked.

"Don't know," Mario said.

"It's in My Old Kentucky Home!"

"Then it must be about to burn up. Call the Fire Department!" Mario announced.

With that, Paul skimmed his paddle across the top of the creek, throwing a sheet of water right at Mario—via Mollie. Shaking off the deluge, she shrank down into the canoe to be out of the path of the return volley.

"Hey, good buddy!" Mario said. "That's never going to put out any fire. Try this!" With that, Mario slapped his paddle on the surface of the water, sprinkling Paul and Mollie ineffectually, but nearly tipping over the canoe.

"Uh, guys." Mollie's voice came muffled from where she huddled in the center of the canoe. "You want to paddle or play?"

"Play!" Mario told her.

"This isn't playing," Paul corrected his friend. "This is work. We have a fire to quench."

In Mollie's opinion, the only fire that was being quenched at that moment was the fire of love. Suddenly it was crystal clear to her that Paul Markham was a jerk—and she'd been a jerk to get a crush on him. She couldn't wait until this dumb canoe ride was over and she was back at camp. She found the thought of being with her sisters a very comforting one. She decided that until she got back she would be safest keeping a low profile among the fire fighters. She scrunched down even more and closed her eyes tightly.

Then another thought occurred to Mollie. They were traveling downstream, without benefit of paddles (the paddles being used for another activity) at quite a clip. There was, in fact, a very strong current carrying them along. Downstream was only one half of the trip. The other half was upstream and that was a lot harder, even if you knew what you were doing in a canoe, which Paul and Mario apparently did not.

Mollie felt very silly huddled on the bottom of the boat, but as long as the water was flying, she thought she ought to stay there.

"Guys," she said, but they didn't answer her. "Paul and Mario, I think there's something we ought to talk about." There was still no answer, but the downpour continued. "Would you boys please stop splashing each other—and incidentally, me—and think for a minute about how we're going to get back upstream?"

"Uh, Mollie," Paul began. But Mollie was too annoyed now about the constant splashing which seemed to be getting worse instead of better.

"Knock off the fire fighting!" she said angrily.

"That's just it, Mollie," Paul said, soothing her. "We did stop it. That's not us. That's rain—a lot of it."

Mollie sat up. The rain was falling steadily. The beautiful clouds that, a few minutes ago, had been playing peek-a-boo with the moon, were now drenching them with a cold driving rain. Mollie looked at the rain. Then she looked at Paul and Mario. They each sat with a paddle poised across the gunwales of the canoe, staring helplessly at the rain.

Fleetingly, Mollie recalled reading somewhere that the stupidest animal in the world is a turkey.

Turkeys, she'd learned, were so dumb that they would go out into a rainstorm and stare up at the rain falling out of the sky until they drowned in it. Paul and Mario were so dumbfounded by the rain that it occurred to Mollie they might drown.

"We've got to stop staring and get to work," Mollie said. "Start paddling."

They each put their paddles in the water on the right-hand side of the boat. The canoe swung to the left.

"Come on, now, one on each side."

The boys both switched to the left hand side. The canoe swung to the right.

"Mario," Mollie said. "You are in the rear, you steer!" she said.

"From the rear?" he asked. "I thought the guy in front did the steering."

"No, a canoe—actually all boats—are controlled from the stern. Where have you been?" she asked, annoyed.

"Landlocked, I guess."

"Okay, now you know better. Paul and I will paddle. You steer."

"How?"

"You're kidding!" was all she could manage.

"I'm afraid not."

"Paul, can you steer?"

"I'm with Mario. I thought I *was* steering it from up here."

"You guys are too much."

"No time for compliments now, Little Sister," Paul said.

"It wasn't actually a compliment," Mollie answered truthfully, wishing he wouldn't call her Little Sister. She could put up with it as long as she had a crush on him, but now ...

"Oooh, that hurt," Paul said.

"Knock off the jokes," Mollie snapped. "They aren't funny now. Look, I'm going to have to steer this thing and I've got to do it from the rear. Mario, you and I are going to change places. That's one thing you try absolutely positively never to do in a canoe, because it's just about guaranteed to tip over and if we tip over we'll be in about ten times the trouble we are in now. I want you to do exactly what I tell you—when I tell you. Hear?"

"Aye, aye, Captain," Mario said.

"Paul, do you know how to ride a bicycle?"

"Of course, I do. I'm no baby," he answered.

Mollie wasn't so sure about that. "Okay, then, you are in charge of balance. During the exchange, the canoe will tip and you're to keep it straight. Remember, though, like on a bicycle, if you tip *too* far in the other direction ..."

"I can handle it," Paul assured her.

"Just like you can handle a canoe?" Mollie asked. She knew it stung. She was glad.

Carefully, she and Mario began their exchange, with her coaxing every move out of Mario and waiting until the canoe stopped rocking after each step.

"Okay, now your other foot. I want you to put it right here. And your hand should go here for balance...."

He stepped, she shifted her weight, moving to the stern.

"Now, I'm going to move upward toward the seat and I want you to shift your weight more to the center of the canoe while—"

Just then, there was a terrifying flash of lightning and crack of thunder. Mollie yowled in fear, grabbing for the seat in the stern. Mario flung himself forward, landing mercifully centered where Mollie had begun. The exchange was complete.

"What was *that*?" Mario asked.

"Lightning," Mollie answered dully. "And I have the funny feeling we're going to see a lot more of it."

"This isn't the safest place to be during an electrical storm," Paul commented.

"That's true," Mollie said. "But right now I don't think we can get to shore. We've got to head back to the campsite."

"How are we going to do that?" Mario asked.

"We're going to do it by paddling like a perfectly matched canoe team. Ready?" Mollie asked.

"Aye, aye, Captain," they answered together.

There was another crack of lightning. "Let's go!" Mollie urged them. They each took a paddle, and while Mollie yelled to them over the rush of the ever-increasing downpour, they tried to follow her instructions.

"Keep the paddle close to the canoe," she called to Paul. "If you paddle way out there, you affect the steering."

"What?" he replied.

Mollie adjusted her steering.

"Mario," she leaned forward and called to him. "Be sure you put the paddle in the water with the flat side cutting through it. Otherwise you're just slowing us down."

Mario stared at his paddle. "Like this?" he asked, sticking it into the water sideways.

"No, Mario, like this," Mollie demonstrated.

"Okay, I'll try, but I should tell you, I think we're taking water in. I'm soaking."

"Not likely we've sprung a leak. I suspect it's from above," Mollie said. "We have to be extra careful about balance if we've got water for ballast."

"Ballast? What's that?"

"Weight. It's used to control how high out of the water a boat rides or to keep it balanced. You can use water for ballast to compensate for un-evenly loaded cargo, but I was just making a joke because if the ballast is sloshing around in the bottom of a canoe, it's not a help, it's bilge."

"Oh," Mario said, and stuck his paddle into the water sideways again.

Not only were they paddling upstream, but they were also paddling into the wind and, therefore, into the storm. It was nearly impossible to see. The only way Mollie could really tell that they were going in the right direction was that it was very hard to paddle. The harder it was to guide the boat, the more certain Mollie was they were correctly aimed.

But that was just one problem. She had no idea how they would know when they'd gotten back to Campsite 15. Most of the creek was lined with a combination of pines and blueberry bushes and there was nothing distinctive Mollie could recall about their own campsite. Even if there were, how on earth would she be able to recognize it if they got there in the pitch black night?

She stared at the horizon, hoping to find some kind of landmark. What she saw instead was a spectacular flash of lightning that illuminated the entire sky for a brief second. There was such a loud crack of thunder immediately afterward that Mollie was sure the lightning had struck something nearby. She strained to see in the darkness. Then there was another flash of lightning and crack of thunder. Mollie squinted in the rain. She could see the top of an old red pine tree tumbling down onto the creek, felled by lightning. She was awfully glad it wasn't tumbling on top of them. She hoped it wouldn't make the creek impassable for a canoe.

"Did you see that?" she said to Paul and Mario.

"See what?" Paul asked.

Figures, Mollie thought. "Oh, nothing. Just that we should keep to the right around that bend." Mollie held her paddle firmly, constantly adjusting for her fellow paddlers' shortcomings. As they rounded the curve in the creek, fighting the current and the wind with every stroke of the paddles, Mollie spotted the branches of the severed treetop sticking out of the water and thanked heaven she'd seen it happen. She knew that she never would have seen it if she hadn't known it was there. Using every ounce of her strength, she maneuvered the canoe around the obstacle, and

they continued on their torturous journey upstream.

The canoe began zigzagging. "Guys, you've got
to paddle together. Otherwise, it's almost impossible to steer."

"I've got my head down against the rain. How
can I tell when he's paddling?" Mario asked.

That was a good question, and one that needed
an answer if they were to get anywhere. Mollie
had an inspiration. "One of two ways. Either I sit
back here and yell 'stroke,' like an old pirate
movie about galley slaves, or we sing." She groped
through her memory to come up with a song they
would all know. "How about 'Vista Stands for Victory'? That should keep us in time with each
other."

Without waiting for agreement from Paul and
Mario, Mollie swung into full tune, choking on the
occasional raindrop. Pretty soon, the boys joined
her in their school fight song:

> *Vista stands for Victory!*
> *So with glory we can be,*
> *With pride we cheer, so all can see*
> *Vista stands for Victory!*

It was a dumb song. Mollie had always known it
was a dumb song, even when she had to learn it
Freshman Week at high school. But it was a song
with a strong, pulsing beat—perfect to paddle by.

"Second verse!" she yelled when they had finished with the first.

"I never learned it!" Paul wailed.

"Sing the first one again!"

And they did—again and again. The rhythm of their paddling was controlled by their singing. They were making headway. Now if only they could find their campsite.

Suddenly, there was another flash of lightning, zig-zagging across the sky. Mollie waited for the thunder, counting.

"One ... two ... three ..." The clash came. "Storm's passing," she told the boys, but she had to yell over the continuing rush of the water.

"Doesn't seem that way to me," Paul called from the bow. "I think it's starting to rain harder!"

It was. And then the wind got worse.

Vista stands for Victory!

The words of the song sounded hollow, but Mollie was determined to get them back to the campsite. That would be her victory, and now it was the only victory that mattered.

So with glory we can be

Mollie tried to wipe the water from her face, but it was impossible. She was straining to see. She thought she'd seen something on the shore ahead, to the left. But that couldn't be. Nobody could see anything in the pitch blackness of the downpour.

With pride we cheer, so all can see

The canoe swung wildly to the right. Mollie paddled desperately to pull it back into the current. Now she was almost certain she'd seen some lights ahead. It had to be a signal. But who could be signaling to them? Then, from the shore, she heard the sweetest sound in the world—for two

more voices, one soprano, one alto, joined them
for the final line of the song.

Vista stands for Victory!

They'd made it!

Chapter 11

"*Nicole? Cindy? Is that you?*" Mollie cried out.

"Yes." Nicole's voice drifted through the rain.

"Who else would be singing such a dumb song?" Cindy shouted, asking the obvious question.

Mollie let out a yell. She'd never been so happy to hear her sisters' slightly off-key voices.

"Stop yelling and keep on steering," Mario snapped.

"Okay, I'll keep steering, you keep singing." They were still twenty feet from the campsite landing area and the battle against the current was not yet won. But they were almost there. Mollie paddled furiously toward shore. The boys did the same. They were as eager as she was to reach dry land—and safety.

She watched as her sisters tried to throw a rope for Paul to catch so he could pull the canoe to shore. It landed six feet short. They drew it in and threw it again. It was closer, but still didn't reach. Mollie smiled to think of the use she'd put that rope to not long ago. It seemed like a lifetime ago.

"Come on, Cindy, try again!" Paul urged. "Think of me as the catcher at home plate, you're the outfielder, and an opponent is about to slide home on a sac fly."

The rope came bounding toward them with new force. Paul reached forward and grabbed it.

"Out at the plate!" he cried, tugging at the rope until it was taut. Mario took the end of it and together, the two of them pulled the canoe to the shore where Cindy and Nicole had the other end of the rope tied to a sturdy tree.

Once the canoe was secured, Paul and Mario stepped off it carefully and then held it, keeping it from tipping, while Mollie stood up and came forward to the shore. As she stepped on shore, Paul and Mario each offered an arm to steady her, but she didn't want their help. She stumbled over to her sisters and nearly collapsed in their arms. At that moment, Mollie could not remember a time in her life when she'd felt happier to see her sisters, or more relieved to be safe. Before she knew it, she was crying. So were they.

"Oh, Mollie, we were so frightened for you," Nicole said.

"So was I," Mollie confessed.

"You were?" Paul asked.

"Of course," Mollie said, a little surprised to find anger at Paul and Mario welling up in her.

"Don't you realize the danger we were in? I mean, we could have tipped over in the middle of the creek and with all that rain, not to mention the lightning, there's really no telling what could have happened to us. And in rain like this—"

"Like what?" Mario asked.

"What do you mean, 'like what?' " Mollie asked, getting angrier.

"I mean 'like what?' " he repeated, holding his hand out, palm up.

Mollie did the same. There was nothing.

"It stopped?" she asked in amazement. "Wow. I guess I was so scared I didn't even notice."

It seemed a bit anticlimactic, but she was glad it had stopped. She'd seen all the rain she cared to see that night. "I don't know about all of you, but I'm ready for some dry clothes."

"That sounds like a pretty good idea," Paul agreed. "Problem is, ours are at my folks' campsite."

"Problem is, good buddy, ours were in our backpacks next to our tent, which we hadn't set up yet, remember?"

"Your total recall is rather depressing," Paul said.

"But accurate," Mario stated.

"Dead accurate," Paul agreed. "I think we have our work cut out for us tonight. I just wish we could cut *it* out." Mario laughed.

Mollie was amazed that they could still be joking about their carelessness. She thought they would have learned their lessons out in the middle of the creek. She shook her head, still surprised that she ever could have thought Paul Markham was the right boy for her.

"Since we can't cut it out, I think we'd better get back to the campsite," Mario said.

"Hey, where *is* your campsite?" Mollie asked, curious. After all, she'd spent a good deal of time trying to find it, and, as it turned out, they'd found her instead.

"We're at number 13—just two campsites up the creek from you."

"And if we'd been upstream from you, instead of the other way around, we never would have seen you, would we?" Mollie asked.

"You got *that* right!" Paul agreed. "When we saw you had a reservation so close to us, we decided to float over here for a visit in my dad's canoe."

"Are you going to float back to your campsite tonight?"

"Nah," Paul said. "I think we've had enough of that thing for now. We'll walk back and then we'll come back tomorrow for the canoe."

"Say, I've got an idea," Cindy said.

"What?" Nicole asked suspiciously.

"As long as Paul and Mario are coming back here tomorrow, why don't we round up the other kids we know in Alta Via this weekend and have a cookout at our site?"

"Hey, great idea!" Mario said.

Paul nodded. "Yeah. I love a party! See you tomorrow. How's seven-thirty?"

"Fine," Nicole said. "Seven-thirty."

"Okay, see you then," Paul said. Mario waved good night, and they turned to leave.

"Hey, how are we going to get word of our party around Alta Via?" Nicole asked once the boys had left.

"I have an idea," Mollie said, remembering her scout friends. Before she could share her idea with her sisters, she heard Paul and Mario still joking.

"Which way is upstream, buddy?" Mario asked Paul.

"It's the way we go using our paddles," Paul said. Mario found this hysterically funny. Nicole, Cindy, and Mollie could hear them laughing uproariously as they walked into the woods. The last the three girls could hear of the boys was a fading chorus of "Vista Stands for Victory."

"What a horrible song," Nicole remarked.

"Whatever made them think of singing it?" Cindy asked.

"It wasn't them," Mollie confessed. "It was me. Those two jerks didn't know anything about canoes. I mean, they didn't even know how to hold their paddles. It was okay as long as we were floating downstream, but when it started raining—"

Suddenly, it all came back to Mollie. Only this time, the real danger of the whole situation came along with it. For a moment, she could see them being swept downstream by a torrential flood, through whitewater, over waterfalls to an unknown fate. She started crying again.

Both Cindy and Nicole reached for her reflexively, comforting her. Her whole body trembled, and she wasn't certain whether the cause was fear or cold.

Nicole took charge of the situation. "That's enough of that for now. Come back to the campsite, get in some warm clothes, sit by a toasty fire, relax, and realize that the danger is behind you now. Once that's done, you can tell us exactly what happened—if you want."

"I will," Mollie said, heading back to campsite 15.

Winston barked happily as soon as he saw Mollie, and Mollie immediately burst out laughing. He was soaking wet.

"Oh, poor Winnie. Let's get a towel for you." She turned toward her tent and said to Nicole, "I can't stand to see him shivering so."

"We'll get a towel for Winston *after* you've dried off and changed," Nicole said sensibly.

"Yeah, Shrimp," Cindy concurred. "If you think Winston looks funny, you should see yourself."

Mollie put her hands on her hips and stared at her sisters. "You guys don't look so hot yourselves, you know, but you were the most beautiful sight in the whole world when I saw you standing by the edge of the creek in the rain a few minutes ago." Mollie didn't want to get too mushy, so she changed the subject to more practical matters. "Okay, first a towel for me, then some dry clothes, then let's take care of Winston."

"That's a good plan, Mollie," Nicole said. "Let's see how much of it we can carry out."

"What does *that* mean?" she asked suspiciously.

"Well, all our clothes were laid out safely in

our tent, but the groundcover leaked and instead of keeping the water out of it, it all got kept *in*. To tell you the truth, I'm not sure we've even got a dry towel in the place—or a dry anything."

"Oh, boy," Mollie said. "Didn't you learn *anything* about camping during all those years you were collecting that incredible knowledge and wisdom you try to bombard me with?"

"I thought I'd picked up a thing or two over the years. What do you know that we don't?" Cindy asked, a little more patient with Mollie than she might normally have been.

"Well, an old camper once told me it's best to put the ground cover inside the tent so it doesn't hold moisture in instead of out."

"Is that what you did in your tent?" Nicole asked.

"Of course. Now let's see if it worked," Mollie said, approaching her tent. She reached the opening flap and pushed it aside. It was completely dark inside, and she couldn't see anything, wet or dry. She stuck her hand in. At first, she felt nothing, but then her hand struck her backpack. "I got something," she announced.

"What?" Nicole asked.

"It's my backpack."

"And?" Cindy asked, unable to stand the suspense.

"It's dry!" Mollie hooted. "Here, give me a flashlight," she asked, extending her hand until Cindy provided the flashlight. Mollie switched it on, and filled her tent with light. "As a matter of fact, everything in here is dry," she told her sisters. "Now, if only I could find my towel."

"It's in the bottom of your backpack," Nicole said.

"How did you know?" Mollie asked.

"We cleaned up your tent with you, remember?"

"Oh, yeah, I do," Mollie said. "Boy, that sure seems like it was an awfully long time ago, though."

"I think it was," Nicole said in her older-and-wiser voice. "It was a very long time ago."

Chapter 12

"*Y*ou didn't happen to bring two towels, did you, Mollie?" Cindy asked.

"Of course." Mollie's muffled voice came from inside her tent. Her grinning face now appeared between the tent flaps. "Why? You want to borrow one?" she asked, feigning surprise.

"Please," Cindy responded eagerly. Mollie handed her the towel through the tent flaps.

"Hey, what about your older, wetter sister?" Nicole asked in mock-protest. "Do you happen to have *another* spare in there for me?" she asked, smiling.

"No, I only brought two towels," Mollie said as she disappeared back into the tent. "But you're welcome to second dibs on this one," she called out loudly enough to be heard through the canvas wall. "Just a second and I'll give it to you." Quickly Mollie got out of her soaking wet clothes and into another one of her outfits. In a few minutes she emerged dry and much warmer than she'd been. "Here's the towel, Nicole," she said, offering it to her sister.

"Thanks, but I don't think it's going to do me much good."

"Why not? It's not that wet," Mollie said.

"Well, I'll dry my hair, I suppose, but all my clothes are soaking wet."

"So, why don't you change into dry ones?" Mollie asked.

"No, Mollie, I mean *all* my clothes are soaking wet—even the ones that are supposed to be dry."

"Oh, no," Mollie said, sympathizing. "Say, would you like to borrow some of mine?" she suggested.

"Yours?" Nicole said. "Why, you're four inches shorter than I am—"

"If you're going to get fussy about size you'll be in trouble, but if you want something dry to wear, I think you'll do okay here," she said, throwing the flap of her tent back in a proprietary welcome.

"Like, what have you got?" Cindy asked suspiciously.

"You want to know if I have something that would fit you, too?" Mollie said.

Cindy nodded, "Sure, I think I do."

"How much clothes did you bring?" Cindy asked.

"Well, you remember I told you about that article in *Seventeen*?"

"Yes, and I remember how I told you you wouldn't need so much clothes, and you agreed."

"I did put away some of the nicer stuff," Mollie

assured her. "But I was right, and so was *Seventeen*, that I'd need plenty of clothes since there's no washing machine here—and no ironing board. Now, let me think about what's going to fit you each the best. Nicole, you're the skinniest, so I guess you can wear my jeans. You want the blue sweatshirt top with the picture of Elvis Presley on it, or would you prefer the pink sweater over my white blouse?"

"Gosh, Mollie," Nicole said, only slightly sarcastically. "I didn't expect to have a choice."

"Hey, what do I get, leftovers?" Cindy asked.

"No, you can have the green shorts and the baggy black sweater—unless you'd prefer the white pants, but I think they'd get too dirty tonight since everything's so wet."

"I can't believe you packed all that stuff!" Nicole said.

"And *I* can't believe I'm actually grateful to *Seventeen* for some article our little sister read in it that told her to do a lot of dumb stuff that actually turned out to be smart. I'll take the green shorts, and if Nicole doesn't want the white blouse, I'll wear that under the black sweater. Okay?"

"It's a deal. I'll take the sweatshirt," Nicole said. I've always loved Elvis Presley—unless. Say, Mollie, you don't happen to have one with Yves Montand on it, do you?"

"No, and I'm fresh out of Louis the Sixteenth sweatshirts, too, but help yourselves to my humble offerings," Mollie said, inviting them both into her tent.

"We will," Cindy assured her, stepping inside.

"Say, I don't suppose you've got any firewood stashed in here, do you? Ours is soaking wet."

"Well, there are just a few logs back there," Mollie said seriously.

"A few logs? I can't believe you, Mollie," Nicole said. "You are the complete general store of campsite 15."

"I guess so," Mollie agreed. "But I only have a small supply of pine cones to start the fire," she said apologetically, stooping to pick up a few from the pile in the corner of the tent. Nicole and Cindy regarded each other in disbelief, than all three sisters burst into laughter.

Mollie stepped out of her tent to give her sisters room to change.

It was strange, Mollie noticed, to suddenly feel so needed by her older sisters. But she realized now, too, how much *she* needed *them*. She had been pretty silly about her independence kick at home and on the way here. She'd been so involved with herself that she'd even forgotten her one responsibility to the group before they left. It wasn't a big job, but it was a job she'd agreed to do, and she hadn't done it. Then, when she set off in search of Paul Markham, she'd been refusing to do another job that was for the good of all three of them. Again, not a giant job, but one that needed to be done.

And there was the canoe ride. At first Mollie had just been trying to get away from her sisters. She'd had romantic images of her and Paul (and Mario) on a moonlight canoe trip, and look what happened. The boys had turned out to be total duds both for the romantic part of her mental image as well as the canoe part. She was still scared when she thought about what might have happened out there on the creek if she hadn't kept her head and used her training.

But then who knows where she would have been if it hadn't been for her sisters? When she had needed them, they were there to bail her out. They had figured out that she was in trouble, and thought of the only way they could help. Then they had done it.

It must have been frightening and frustrating waiting on the shore with their flashlights, only hoping it would help. Now things seemed to have turned around a bit. Her sisters had goofed setting up their tent so everything they had brought on the trip was wet. She had come to *their* rescue.

Cindy emerged from Mollie's tent, rubbing the towel on her still damp hair, but wearing Mollie's dry clothes.

"Boy, does that ever feel better," she said, giving Mollie an affectionate hug.

"You're not going to go mushy on me just because I packed a lot of clothes, are you?" Mollie asked.

"Nope, but considering the differences in our sizes, I'm going to thank the designers for the baggy look," Cindy exclaimed, flopping her arms and shaking the over-size sweater.

"Not bad," Mollie said. "I don't think it'll get you on the cover of *Seventeen*, though."

"Oh, dear. Will it get me some help clearing the

wet wood out of the fire area so we can start a new fire and get warm?"

"Am I on kindling again?" Mollie asked.

"Only if you can get the stuff from the corner of your tent to the fireplace in less than two hours this time."

"I think I can swing it. Where's the kindling that I brought back?"

"In our tent," Cindy said.

Mollie nodded and walked over to her sisters' tent. Inside was as much of a mess as they had promised. Absolutely everything except one sleeping bag was soaking wet—floating, in fact, on a lake formed by their groundcover. Some help that had been. Mollie shone her light around until she found the kindling. It was floating, too. She gave up that idea.

"I think we're going to have to make do with the dry wood in my tent," Mollie said. "I've got a copy of *Young Miss* we could burn for kindling."

"Great idea," Cindy agreed. "But don't burn *Seventeen*. You never can tell when that magazine will come in handy!"

"Yeah, in case I want to use some of the decorating ideas for my tent."

"No, Mollie, I think your tent is just about perfect as it is," Cindy said.

Cindy and Mollie were laughing when Nicole emerged from Mollie's tent, dry, carrying two dry logs.

"Okay, fire time!" Nicole announced.

Quickly, Mollie and Cindy tore up the magazine while Nicole carefully laid the wood on. They added the pine cones to the pile. When Nicole was satisfied that it was the best they could do, she produced a match and lit the fire.

"It's too bad those scouts aren't around," Mollie said.

"What scouts?" Cindy asked.

"The scouts I met on my adventure in the woods looking for kindling. Whenever you need anything done, all you have to do is to ask who needs a badge in that particular skill."

"Is that how you got your pants mended?" Cindy teased.

"Yeah, well, it was three poor girls' Level-One Badges. I signed the papers, too. They'll get the badges next week."

"And then their mothers' are going to have to sew it on their uniforms for them," Nicole said.

"Unless they want to attach them with natural fibers," Cindy said, giggling.

"Speaking of badges, Mollie, you certainly earned one in canoeing tonight. Tell us about what happened," Nicole said.

"You mean with those two duds?" Mollie asked.

Her sisters nodded. And Mollie told them everything as they warmed themselves around the fire. She told them about floating downstream, about the water fight, about the rain, the lightning, about how Paul and Mario were totally helpless, and about how she was almost too busy to be scared.

"Until I saw the lightning strike the tree. I couldn't believe that. It was incredible."

"We saw it from here and it frightened us. You were much closer. You must have been terrified."

"I was." Mollie shivered at the memory.

"Tell us what started you singing," Nicole prodded.

"Well, those two goof-offs couldn't paddle at the same time and it was impossible for me to keep the canoe on course. We kept swinging wildly. I had to get them paddling in unison. So I told them we were going to have to sing to coordinate our strokes. I remembered what you had said in the car about 'Alouette,'" Mollie explained. "And the school song was the first thing that we would all know that came into my mind."

"I've got to tell you something, Mollie," Nicole said. "There Cindy and I were, on the shore, wondering how on earth we would ever be able to see you through the pouring rain, and when I heard that awful singing, I thought it was the greatest sound in the world."

"Yeah? You think I should join the choir?" Mollie asked.

"Well," Nicole hesitated. "On second thought . . ."

Mollie tossed some leaves at her sister and then said, "I have something to say to you guys. I owe you both an apology. I was really acting like a jerk earlier today. I mean, I have no excuse for forgetting to feed the animals and for behaving the way I was. I'm really sorry. I got so hung up on being independent that I forgot about my responsibilities."

"I think you showed us tonight, rather effectively, that you know how to be responsible, too," Nicole said.

"I guess so. And, I also learned what can happen when somebody is completely irresponsible."

"What do you mean?" Cindy asked.

"Paul and Mario," Mollie said, while unsuccessfully stifling a yawn.

"Tired?" Nicole asked.

"Beat." Mollie confessed. "I'm so tired, I could probably sleep standing up right now."

"You may have to," Cindy said.

"Huh?"

"Our tent, remember? It's full of water. We all have to sleep in your little tent."

"That is," Nicole said, "assuming you don't want to make yourself another hammock."

"Well, that'll be cozy," Mollie said, ignoring her sister's joke. "It's a good thing we're friends, isn't it?" She added cheerfully, "It's going to be awfully close quarters."

Chapter 13

"*Hey, are you awake?*" *It was Cindy.*

Mollie opened one eye. She closed it again.

"C'mon. I saw. I know you're awake."

"What makes you so sure?"

"Because the sun is shining. And even if you're not awake, you should be," Cindy said. "Just because you went for a spin in a canoe last night is no reason to sleep the day away. Breakfast is almost cooking and the morning awaits you, Your Majesty."

"Who, me?" Mollie asked.

"Yeah, you. Besides, we need your help hanging all the wet stuff out to dry in the sun. Otherwise, Nicole and I will spend the rest of the day wearing your clothes and another night sharing a sleeping bag in your tent. Not that we aren't grateful, mind you. It's just that the clothes are not quite our style, you know?"

"You mean, you think you look too much like a well-dressed freshman?"

"I wouldn't actually put it that way, Mollie," Cindy said with a smirk.

"What's for breakfast?" Mollie asked.

"Nicole said something about making what she calls *crêpes sauvages*."

"What's that?"

"Flapjacks," Cindy told her. "Plain old American pancakes which the French seem to have a fancy name for."

"And if the French have a fancy name for something, you can bet plain old American Nicole will use it," Mollie said.

"Yes, and speaking for myself, if Nicole cooks it, plain old American Cindy will eat it."

"Me too," Mollie said, crawling out of the tent and taking a deep breath of fresh air. "What a gorgeous day, a perfect day to sit around the campsite and veg out."

"Forget that, Mollie," Cindy said sternly. "We're going for a hike as soon as we eat breakfast."

"Hike? How come all you ever want to do is something?"

"Huh?"

Mollie thought about what she'd said for a second and then realized how silly it sounded. She tried again. "I mean, how come you never want to do nothing?"

Cindy decided to play dumb. "Double negatives will get you nowhere, Mollie. It's not time to not eat your breakfast. You don't want to be no victim of no starvation, don't you?"

Mollie looked at Cindy quizzically. "No," she answered. "I mean, yes." That didn't sound right either. "I mean, I'm hungry. Are the pancakes ready yet?"

"Are you ready to hang up wet clothes and then go for a hike after breakfast?"

"Okay already," Mollie answered, resigned. She figured that once Cindy had made up her mind, as she apparently had, that she was going to be pack leader, there was nothing to do except follow, unless she wanted to get into the same kind of mess she'd been in yesterday. She decided to sound more cooperative before she was assigned some baby job. "I mean, *great* idea!"

Nicole appeared at the opening of Mollie's tent. *"Bonjour, ma petite sœur!"* she said cheerfully.

"Morning," Mollie answered. Even when Mollie knew how to answer her sister in French, she often didn't. She didn't like to encourage her. "What's this I hear about pancakes?" Mollie asked.

"Crêpes sauvages, you mean," Nicole corrected her. "They'll be ready in about ten minutes—if I don't burn them on the first try."

"Oh, I remember the last time you tried cooking something more complicated than hot dogs on a campfire—" Mollie began, teasing.

"I try to forget, thank you very much."

"Wasn't that the time the forest rangers came over to see if the campfire was blazing out of control?" Cindy teased.

"Uh, like I said, I forget," Nicole lied. Mollie and Cindy laughed.

"Okay, here's the plan," Mollie said, sounding as

much like Cindy as she could. "I'm going down to the creek to wash up and brush my teeth. I'll bring back a couple of extra buckets of water, you know, just in case," she said, glancing meaningful at the frying pan.

"Sounds like a good idea," Cindy said. "Just in case we have a fire like the one you started at home in the kitchen last time Mom and Dad left us alone, remember?"

"Sorry, I don't remember that at all," Mollie said. "But it sounds a little like the time you got a concussion while you were sailing because you didn't know what you were doing. Remember that?"

"No," Cindy said. "Doesn't sound at all familiar."

"Must be the Lewis syndrome," Nicole said. "None of us can remember our greatest failures."

"Seems pretty sensible to me," Cindy said.

"Me, too," Mollie concurred. "Okay, so I *won't* bring the fire brigade back from the creek. I'll just brush my teeth and see you back here in a couple of minutes."

"Don't go anywhere in that canoe," Cindy warned with a laugh.

"Don't worry," Mollie promised, heading for the water. "I don't think I'll get near a canoe for a very long time."

Cindy and Nicole returned to the campfire to stir the embers and start breakfast.

Mollie skipped happily down to the creek. It flowed smoothly and serenely. As she gazed at it, it was hard to believe that just last night it had been so terrifying. Today the water was calm and almost crystal clear.

Mollie washed up quickly because the water was icy cold. She was also in a hurry to get back and help her sisters. It was a funny thing about sisters, she thought. Most of the time they were just there, not good, not bad. Some of the time they were awful, bossy tattletales. And then, every once in a while, sisters were wonderful. Since right now was one of those times, Mollie didn't want to miss a minute of it. As soon as she was done, she hurried back up the hill to the campfire.

"Anything caught fire yet?" she asked.

"Just the wood," Cindy told her. "And that was some accomplishment. Most of the wood around here is still pretty wet from the rain."

"Well, so are your clothes," Mollie reminded her. "While we wait for our *petit déjeuner*—that's French for breakfast in case you happen to be the Lewis sister who took Spanish—why don't we get to work on your wardrobe?"

"Good idea," Cindy agreed.

Nicole was left to struggle with the campfire. The trick to making flapjacks was getting the heat fairly evenly distributed under the frying pan. She knew perfectly well that it would be a lot easier to get the box of cereal from the food storage case, but the challenge of campfire cooking was great. She really wanted to master it. As she stirred the ingredients together, she imagined herself taking a romantic camping trip through France, creating gourmet meals over a campfire. What she couldn't see herself doing was dishing out corn flakes in the middle of the French countryside.

She put some butter on the griddle and listened to the sizzle. It sounded right. Carefully, she ladled batter onto the pan.

Mollie and Cindy lugged all of Cindy and Nicole's belongings out of the big tent and carried the soggy mess to the clearing where they could spread everything out in the sun.

"One piece of good news here," Mollie remarked.

"What's that?"

"Well, since the two of you didn't pack anywhere near enough clothes, there isn't so much to dry."

"You mean it's a good thing the water didn't leak into your tent instead of ours?"

"Absolutely," Mollie said. "If it had, you guys wouldn't have had enough clothes to share with me the way I had to share with you, and they certainly wouldn't be as stylish."

"I suppose there's something to that. But for now let's concentrate on figuring out how we're going to use this little patch of sunshine to our best advantage."

The two of them struggled to lay out the sleeping bag and clothes, but no matter how they did it, most of the things were in the shade. Mollie kept thinking that there must be a solution to the problem. There didn't seem to be.

"Hey, I've got an idea," Cindy announced.

"Take this stuff to a Laundromat?" Mollie suggested.

"No, my idea is to make some more use of your macrame skills."

"Aha! The famous old macrame laundry line?" Mollie asked.

"Something like that, but a little simpler. How about we just tie the rope from tree to tree and hang the stuff on it?"

"It's a deal," Mollie agreed. "I'll get the rope from the creek." In a few minutes she was back. "Boy, this rope sure has been put to use on this trip. Now, for my famous plant hanger . . ."

"Just tie it to the tree, Mollie. Save the arts and crafts for Christmas."

They each took an end of the rope and quickly assembled a clothes line. When they finished hanging the clothes, they returned to the campfire.

"Breakfast ready yet?" Cindy asked.

"Depends," Nicole said.

"Depends on what?" Cindy asked suspiciously.

"Depends on how you feel about perfectly golden brown flapjacks," Nicole answered.

"I love 'em," Cindy said.

"Then breakfast isn't ready yet," Nicole said. "Now if you like mostly black but partially golden brown, as in one corner, then breakfast is ready." She pointed to a small stack of charcoal-colored flapjacks.

"I think I'll wait for the next batch," Cindy said.

"Hey, Winston!" Mollie called. "You hungry boy?" She tossed the burned flapjacks to him. He stepped toward them, curious. He eyed the offered treat, sniffed it, and walked away, looking as though he'd been insulted at the suggestion.

"Maybe he thinks they need butter and syrup," Nicole said.

"Yeah, and maybe he thinks we should take them home to the cats," Cindy suggested. "When's the next batch going to be ready?"

Nicole glanced at the griddle. "I think it almost is," she said, turning over the flapjacks. "Hey! Look at this!"

Her sisters gathered around her to see what the excitement was about. They stared in amazement, for there, sitting on the griddle, were four perfectly golden flapjacks.

"Think your luck'll hold while the other side cooks?" Mollie asked.

"Luck? You think this is luck? What you're looking at is years of training coming to fruition."

"Huh?" Mollie said.

"I think what she means is that she's learned something from those years of burned flapjacks."

"And I think you're right," Nicole admitted. "Here, one each, and one for Winston, out of this batch. No telling what's going to happen with the next batch, so enjoy."

She dealt out the flapjacks to her eager and hungry sisters, and they lathered them with butter and syrup and ate contentedly. By the third batch, Nicole had perfected her system. "Well, I could go on making these all day, but I think it's time for that hike," she said.

"I'm ready," Cindy said.

"Me too," Mollie agreed. "But first I think I hear an answer to a problem coming through the woods."

Cindy and Nicole looked at each other in confusion. All they could hear were off-key young voices singing "Found a Peanut."

"What are you talking about Mollie?" Nicole asked.

"Hang on," Mollie said, running towards the sound in the woods. Her sisters waited impatiently for a few minutes and then, to their surprise, Mollie emerged from the woods, followed by a squad of four uniformed scouts.

"Nicole, Cindy," she said. "I'd like you to meet my rescuers from last night—or at least some of them."

"Oh, the great sewing job," Cindy joked. One of the girls blushed. Cindy could tell right away that it wasn't something she should joke about, and she tried to smooth the situation. "So *creative!*" she said admiringly.

"Thank you," the scout responded.

"How come you're out hiking so early?" Nicole asked.

"We're foraging for berries for our breakfast," a pigtailed scout answered her. "Our leaders have offered to show us how to make berry jam if we bring back enough food, but, to tell you the truth, it's not the berry season and we haven't found much. Isn't the Commissary near here?" she asked. "We're hungry!"

"Not far," Mollie told her. "But I think we can work something out."

"Like what?" the scout asked suspiciously.

"Well, we need a little help spreading a message through the Park to everyone here who goes to our school—think you could do that for us?"

"Well, sure, but what's in it for us?" a petite brunette challenged.

"Flapjacks!" Mollie announced cheerfully. The scouts looked at each other. It only took a second for them to make a decision.

"It's a deal—whatever you want us to do, Mollie, it's a deal!"

Nicole took out the ingredients and assembled another batch of batter. While she cooked for the scouts, Mollie explained what they wanted them to do and Cindy drove over to the registration office to put together a list of the Vista kids and their campsites. Within half an hour, all instructions and flapjacks had been dispensed. Everybody seemed happy with their end of the deal.

"This'll be a snap," one of the scouts said. "Much easier than finding berries. And I don't even think the leaders will mind that we're gone. There are a few girls who think that the leaders sent us off on an impossible task just to get rid of us."

"I can't imagine why," Mollie said, recalling the mayhem at the campsite the night before.

"Neither can I," said the scout, mopping up the last of her syrup with the last of her flapjacks. "Well, anyway, we'll carry messages for you anytime as long as you keep feeding us."

"I'll keep that in mind," Nicole said, shaking her head in amazement at how much food the four girls had consumed.

As soon as the scouts finished breakfast, they began to gather plates to take them to the creek to wash.

"You don't have to do that," Mollie said. "We have to do our own anyway. We'll clean up." The scouts thanked Mollie and then thanked Nicole profusely for breakfast. They assured the sisters their messages would be delivered faithfully, and they disappeared into the woods—as silently as they had come—still singing painfully off-key.

"Now it's time for our hike—as soon as we finish washing up together," Mollie said.

"You know what, Nicole?" Cindy said.

"What?"

"I think Mollie's getting the hang of this team-work idea, don't you?"

"We'll see," Nicole said.

Mollie rolled her eyes and let out a sigh.

Chapter 14

"*Pace yourself, Mollie,*" Cindy told her. "*You're* going too fast. If you try to keep that up, you'll be completely burned-out before we're halfway up the hill."

Mollie took a deep breath and kept on walking.

"Mollie, I know what I'm talking about." There was a note of irritation in her voice.

Once again, Mollie found herself getting tired of her sisters. They both always seemed to think that everything they did or said was right, and everything anyone else said or did—Mollie, for instance—was wrong. She was all set to explode at Cindy and tell her she didn't need her advice when she was suddenly flooded with the image of her sisters standing on shore the night before, waving their flashlights and singing. She had needed them then. Now she realized it was more than possible that the superathlete of the family,

Cindy, might know what she was talking about. Mollie slowed down.

"How's this?" she asked.

"Better," Cindy said.

It *was* better, too. She wasn't going so quickly, but she wasn't getting so tired, either. She wasn't, for instance, too tired to notice how beautiful the area was. After a while, though, she was running out of breath again.

"I can't wait till we get to the top and sit down. It's going to feel great!"

"I wouldn't mind sitting down myself," Nicole said. "Why don't we look for a clearing where we can have our lunch?"

"But we're so close to the top!" Cindy complained. "You two are really out of shape, aren't you."

"I thought we were doing all right," Nicole said.

"Sure, you're doing all right, but you're not doing well. You both need to exercise so you can get in shape and stay in shape. That way, the next time we come to Alta Via we can take a ten-mile hike instead of a wimpy two-mile one."

"Doesn't she sound like a recruiter for a health spa?" Mollie asked Nicole. " 'If you join now, a friend can join for half the price.' "

" 'But only if we act on this special offer today,' " Nicole said.

Cindy got into the spirit of things. "And that's the deal," she said, mimicking a fast-talking salesman. "If you call now, right now, you can join for half price and a friend can join for twice the price. That's two for the price of two-and-a-half. What a deal, folks. This offer will not be repeated!"

"I should hope not," Nicole said.

"And the fourth person who calls tonight will receive this special, one-time bonus," Mollie continued for Cindy. "One totally exhausting, completely exasperating, fully excruciating climb to the top of a mountain, complete with an exotic native guide." Mollie was rather pleased with herself and what she thought was a clever little speech, when they came around the final bend leading to the top of the mountain, Cindy finished the spiel for her.

"—Who will provide an exegesis of the exhilarating view from said extreme summit."

"Exegesis?" Nicole repeated with a puzzled look.

"Yeah, it means explanation or analysis of something. Don't you guys learn *anything* in French class?"

Cindy's sisters were still giggling when they took the few remaining steps to the peak of the mountain. They emerged from the cover of the forest and stopped, silent, too awed even to sit down.

"Wow," was all Mollie could say. She found herself gazing out across miles and miles of rolling green treetops, and beyond them, smoothly curving hills. The sky was a glorious blue, dotted here and there with soft puffs of clouds.

"This is something," Nicole agreed.

"See? I told you there was no point in stopping for lunch before we got here. I came here on a class outing last year, I just couldn't believe it, either. I mean, you just can't get a view like that anywhere. Not even from the top of the Eiffel Tower, I bet."

"Shhh, Cindy," Nicole said. "I just want to look."

"Okay, okay," Cindy said, secretly pleased that she had been able to surprise her sisters with the spectacular view.

Nicole stared out across the mountains, silently absorbing the scenery. Mollie retrieved her sketch pad and her pencils from her pack and sat on a rock, drawing, trying to capture the absolute beauty of the place.

Cindy, meanwhile, opened the backpacks, which held their picnics, and laid out lunch on top of a flat rock.

"Dinner is served," she said. Her sisters pulled themselves away from the view reluctantly.

"Did you see that eagle?" Mollie asked Nicole.

"Yes, it was gorgeous, gliding through the sky so peacefully. Did you see the waterfall?"

"No, where?"

"It's over there, on the smaller mountain." Nicole told her, pointing to a mountain to their left.

Mollie put down her sketch pad and reached for a sandwich. She turned to Cindy. "Is it possible that I can see Santa Barbara from here?"

"Sure," Cindy said. "It's west and a little bit north of here, that way." She pointed to where Mollie had seen signs of civilization, black smoke and gray smog. "And the ocean is just beyond it."

"Can we see the sunset from here?" Mollie asked.

"Sure, if you don't mind missing the party we're giving."

"Oh, wow. I almost forgot. We're having a party tonight, aren't we?"

Cindy and Nicole each took a sandwich and Cindy handed out sodas to both of her sisters before opening one for herself.

"Yes, and from the sound of your eager messengers, it should be fairly well-attended," Nicole said.

"Yeah, those scouts are great, aren't they?" Mollie said.

"Well, they're certainly an enthusiastic crowd. But I wonder, do you think their leaders are starving them? I've never seen anybody attack the food quite the way they did."

"Well, you've probably never eaten slumgullion," Mollie responded.

"No. You're right. I haven't. Is that what you allegedly had for supper before you got back to the campsite and wolfed down two hot dogs last night?" Nicole asked.

"The very same stuff," Mollie told her.

"I think I understand now," Nicole said. "Aside from lacking cooking skills, they seem like a nice bunch of girls. You think they'll be able to find everyone?"

"Sure. We gave them a list of names and campsites from the registration office," Mollie assured her.

"Will the scouts get badges in Invitations for doing this?" Cindy asked.

"Nope. In Communications."

"Well, whatever, it was a great idea to ask them. We would have been exhausted going from campsite to campsite, and we wouldn't have been able to take this hike," Cindy said.

"Right, instead we got exhausted climbing a mountain."

"Ah, but what a mountain," Cindy said.

"Yes, it is beautiful here," Mollie agreed.

By now Nicole was gazing dreamily at the horizon, completely lost in her own thoughts and ignoring her sisters' banter.

Cindy started to say something to her, but Nicole seemed to be on another planet.

"I think it's time to get Mademoiselle Lewis back to the campsite, Mollie," Cindy said. "All this beauty seems to be getting to her. We don't want her to forget how to cook for us, do we?"

"Certainly not!" Mollie said. "Besides, it's time to check in with the scouts to see exactly how many people are coming to our pow-wow tonight." Mollie stood up and began cleaning up from their picnic.

"I think it's time to go back," Nicole said. Her sisters stared at her for a second and then burst into laughter. "Did I say something funny?" Nicole asked.

"Yes. I mean, no. I mean, oh, forget it," Cindy said. "Come on, Nicole. You're absolutely right. It's time to head back to the campsite. Now everybody make sure to pick everything up and put the papers in the backpack. Crumbs and stuff that will be eaten by birds may be left behind. Everything else, and I mean *everything*, must be cleaned up."

"Sounds like the drill sergeant is back on active duty," Mollie said, frowning.

Cindy winked at her, and together they gathered and repacked everything.

"Come on, guys," Cindy said when they were done. "Wait'll you see how beautiful the mountain is on the way down."

"It bet it looks even better when you're not climbing it," Mollie said.

"Yeah, let's go have a party!" She gave a little jump and started skipping down the mountainside.

Chapter 15

"*E*verything's completely dry," Cindy said, stowing the last of her clothes in the tent.

"Yes. Luckily. I wouldn't have wanted to display all our damp clothes during the party tonight," Nicole said.

"Let's take down the drying line. Then we can forget about last night's disastrous rainstorm completely," Cindy suggested.

"I'm not so sure we *should* forget all about the rainstorm," Nicole said. "After all, it seems to have taught us something."

The two sisters walked back toward the clearing where their clothes had recently been hanging. Cindy shinnied up one of the pine trees and, balancing perilously on a skinny branch, reached out to untie one of Mollie's knots.

"You mean about how not to put the groundcover outside the tent?" she asked.

"Well, I was thinking more in terms of mutual respect. Mollie was acting like a bratty little kid on the way up here, but she certainly showed maturity later with the boys in the canoe. And then, to be honest, you and I were being rather bratty when we pulled all those stunts on Mollie—"

"You're not going to suggest that I stop playing practical jokes, are you?" Cindy asked. She was nervous about the turn this conversation seemed to be taking.

"Of course not, Cindy. As long as I'm not the victim of one."

"Never," Cindy said with a sigh of relief.

"Here's the rope from this side. You start reeling it in. I'll get the other side." She climbed down from the tree. "Anyway," she went on. "I don't think you can have mutual respect among three people. I think mutual means there are two people."

Nicole wrapped the rope around her arm. "Okay, Merriam-Webster, what do you think you should call mutual respect among three people?"

Cindy walked across the clearing and climbed up the other pine tree. It was harder to get a foothold this time. Her sneaker kept slipping along the smooth bark. Nicole came to her aid, offering her hands as a stirrup, hoping Cindy wouldn't break one of her nails. Cindy finally reached the rope and had it undone in a matter of seconds. She plopped back down to the ground, and said, "*Tritual* respect," answering Nicole's question.

"Very cute," Nicole said, groaning.

"Wow, I can't believe fifteen people are actually

coming to our party," Mollie said. "What do we have to do to get ready?"

"Not much," Nicole said. "No house cleaning, since this party's taking place in the great outdoors. Then, since it's strictly a bring-your-own food party, I think we're off the hook on that, too. Our job, then, is to prepare a good fire and have a good time."

"Boy, I'm ready for that!" Mollie said.

"Such enthusiasm," Cindy remarked. "Does that mean that you haven't been having a good time so far this weekend?"

"Oh, not at all," Mollie said brightly. "It's been a barrel of fun."

"You mean like a barrel rolling over Niagara Falls, huh?" Cindy asked.

"Yeah, something like that," Mollie said. "Say, I just thought of something we need to do. We don't have any kindling for the fire yet."

"Congratulations, you get the job," Cindy told her. To her amazement, Mollie stood up with no argument and set off to pick up some little sticks and pine cones. She returned five minutes later with a handful of twigs and their first two guests, Paul and Mario.

"Hi, guys," Cindy said.

"Good evening." They both bowed politely.

"How'd you boys sleep last night, soaking wet?" Mollie asked adding the kindling to the pile of logs in the fireplace and lighting the fire.

"Actually, we were completely dry and toasty warm," Paul said.

"How'd you manage that?"

"We tossed in the towel and went to a local motel."

"You cheaters!" Mollie accused them.

"You bet!" Paul agreed. "We had actually had quite enough of the great outdoors by the time we got back to our campsite and the sight of everything we owned totally drenched was simply too much for us. My folks' tent was full of water, too. So off we went to the Ko-Zee Kabins right down the road. Then, this morning, we went to the Laundromat and what you see before you is the result of a couple of hours of washing, drying, and folding."

"But we couldn't have done it without the help of a couple of our classmates who happened to be there at the same time. We now present Elaine and Jessica!"

Two girls from Cindy's class emerged from the darkness to join the group at the campfire.

"You girls washed all their clothes and stuff?" Mollie asked.

"We did," Elaine told her.

"You boys are totally helpless without girls to save you, aren't you."

"You got it, Little Sister," Paul said. "So, Elaine, save me!" he cried, pretending to faint. Elaine ran over to his side and held him up. "I'm having trouble breathing," he said.

"I already heard the one about mouth-to-mouth resuscitation, Paul. You're on your own now."

She let go of him and he fell to the ground, doing a pretty good imitation of someone struggling to breathe, only in his case, he was having trouble because he was laughing so hard.

Mollie had to laugh, too. Paul actually *was* fun to be around. He was totally straightforward about his shortcomings and he was always so eager to have a good time that he usually succeeded. But he still wasn't Mollie's idea of a boyfriend.

"Is this campsite 15?" came a voice through the darkness.

"Yes," Nicole said. "Who's that?"

"It's Duncan James and Sam Wellington. Some kid came and told us about a party for Vista students here. Is that right?"

"Hey, great!" Nicole said, welcoming them. They were in her class. "Come on up to our campfire. Did you bring something to eat?"

"Hi, Nicole. Yeah, we brought our own food," Sam said. "But if we'd known you were the hostess, we might not have. I've heard you're a fabulous cook."

Nicole was flattered, but she didn't know what to say.

"She is," Cindy answered for her. "Particularly if you like charcoaled flapjacks, right Mollie?"

"Cindy's right," Mollie echoed. "It's a good thing you brought your own food."

"Speaking of cooking," Paul said. "I think that fire needs some work. Is there more wood around?"

"Sure, there's some over there," Mollie said, pointing to their woodpile.

"Good. Then why don't you put some logs on and build the fire up enough for me to roast my tube steak?"

"Tube steak?" Mollie asked, too curious about the idea of such a thing to notice how he'd conned her into getting more wood while he sat down. She plunked a log on the fire and asked again. "What's a tube steak?"

"A hot dog, of course," he answered. "In my family we don't call them fancy things like *chiens chauds*. We just call them plain old tube steaks."

Pretty soon nearly everybody at the party had something cooking on the fire, mostly hot dogs, some hamburgers, one minute steak, one cheese dog. The fire glowed warmly, illuminating the faces of those gathered around it. When new guests arrived—and six more did—they were given places around the campfire to cook their dinner.

"Hello, everybody!" a new voice came from the woods. It was Garrett Ellis, a junior from Vista. "Boy, I never saw so many familiar faces in such an unfamiliar place. Is the whole school here for the weekend?" he asked, joining the diners at the campfire.

"No, but an awful lot of us are, and when the invitations to a campfire party are issued by such a fetching bunch of messengers, well, how could any of us say no?" Paul asked.

"I brought my cassette player. How about some music to really get this party going," Garrett offered.

Cries of "great," "sure," "turn it on," answered him. Soon the music was blaring, and the party was really rolling.

As far as Mollie, Cindy, and Nicole were concerned, their party was a huge success. Everything was going smoothly. Everybody was behaving and enjoying themselves, and, most important for the hostesses, the sisters didn't have to do anything but have a good time. The guests chatted noisily about what they'd been doing while they were camping out in the park. Eventually, talk turned to Paul, Mario, and Mollie's wild canoe trip of the night before, with Paul telling an embellished version of the story.

"So there I was," he told the guests, "paddling quietly and smoothly along the creek like a good boy, having myself a nice old time in a very tippy canoe when all of a sudden two things happened. First, the sky opened up and started dumping water on me and into my boat, and then I found myself in the hands of a slave driver." He pointed to Mollie. " 'Stroke!' she cries. So I did. 'Not that way!' she yells. 'Like this!' she tells me," he said, demonstrating his sideways paddling method. "And as if that weren't good enough, we—that's Mario and me—we were ordered to entertain her, like with music. Now, we didn't have anything nice like Garrett's cassette player with us, and even if we had it wouldn't play the kind of music Mollie likes. Her choice was 'Vista Stands for Victory.' Can you believe it?"

Paul burst out laughing as soon as he finished the story. Mario joined him and within a few seconds, everybody at the campfire was laughing hysterically, glancing curiously at Mollie.

Mollie thought she was going to die of humiliation. When it didn't happen, she began hoping the ground would open and swallow her up. She couldn't believe that she could have single-handedly gotten Paul out of such a horrible situation only to have him tell the story in a way that made fun of her. She was near tears when she heard him say "... and then she wanted us to do the second verse!" The kids roared with laughter.

Cindy glanced at her sister and saw how upset she looked. "Hey, Paul," she chided, "why don't you tell everyone what *really* happened?"

"Aww, come on. This is so much fun," he said.

"Come on, Paul," Nicole prodded.

"Okay, okay. What really happened is that Mario and I were completely helpless in that canoe. The only one who knew what she was doing was Mollie Lewis. And not only that, she also knew how dangerous the situation was *and* she knew how to get us out of it. While we struggled to paddle, Mollie figured out the only way to keep us paddling in unison was to sing, and sure enough, that dumb song did the trick. So now you know the *real* story. We might not be here at all to tell it. Right, Little Sister?" he asked.

Mollie was too embarrassed to say anything at all.

Paul spoke again. "Now how about a rousing round of 'Vista Stands for Victory' to honor Mollie Lewis—a girl who knows how to paddle her own canoe?"

Then, to Mollie's total astonishment and pleasure, everybody at the campfire stood up and sang one verse of "Vista Stands for Victory." When they sat down, Mollie remained standing to speak to her friends.

"Thank you for that beautiful rendition of a truly awful song."

Just then, a very familiar voice came from the edge of the campsite.

"Hello! Anybody home?"

"I know that voice," Cindy said.

"So do I," Nicole piped in.

"Dad!" Mollie yelled, running toward her father.

"Hi, baby," he said, emerging into the circle of light from the campfire and dropping two bags to hug her.

"What are you doing here? Is Gramma okay?" Mollie asked, wondering what had brought her father to their campsite.

"Everything's fine. Why don't you help your mother and grandmother get the other things from the car?"

"Gramma Lewis is here?" Cindy asked, astonished.

"When she learned that we were missing a camping weekend to be with her, we couldn't stop her from coming. So we decided to come along, too. She was a little worried about you three girls being here alone, but from the looks of everything, you're doing fine without us."

"Gramma!" Mollie greeted her with a big hug. "We thought you were in pain!"

"So'd the doctor and that's what he told your parents. But the only pain was in my neck—and it was caused by the hospital. I just wanted to get out of there!"

"Well, it's great to see you, Gramma," Cindy

said, hugging her, too. "Come sit by the campfire and enjoy the party."

"I think I will," Gramma Lewis said settling herself down comfortably on a log.

With everyone's help, the Lewises' camping gear was quickly removed from the car and the tents pitched. When that was done, Mr. and Mrs. Lewis joined the kids and Gramma Lewis at the campfire.

"S'mores anyone?" Cindy asked.

"For everyone?" Paul asked.

"Get yourself a stick for the marshmallow and you can have as many as you want."

Nicole, in the meantime, was cooking hot dogs for her parents and grandmother. After they had their main course, they joined in on the S'mores.

"This is the life," Gramma Lewis said.

"You're really something, Gramma," Mollie said in an admiring tone. "I mean, just a couple of days ago you broke your arm, and now here you are, just another one of the kids around the campfire."

"Well," Gramma said, "to tell you the truth, this camper is getting a little tired. I think I'm ready for my sleeping bag."

The partygoers all knew how to take a hint when they heard one. One by one, they stood up, thanked the Lewises and left for their own campsites. As the last of them left, Nicole, Cindy, and Mollie could hear traces of "Vista Stands for Victory" being hummed quietly.

"Why on earth are your friends singing such a horrible song, girls?" Gramma Lewis asked.

"I have no idea," Cindy said innocently.

The three girls exchanged a tritual laugh.

Chapter 16

"*I* can hardly believe what a wonderful job you girls have done," Mrs. Lewis said the next morning while she and Nicole were serving breakfast to the rest of the family. They were having perfectly grilled French toast. "Didn't you have any trouble?"

"Oh, a little," Cindy said casually.

"But it all worked out all right," Nicole assured them.

"Well, I can see that," Mr. Lewis said. "And I can also see that it was a good decision to let you girls do this alone. I can't remember the last time I saw you three getting along so well. You've certainly proven that you can go camping by yourselves, and you can do it again anytime you'd like."

"Uh, thanks, Dad," Cindy said.

"But we think once is enough," Nicole said.

"Yeah, once in a *lifetime*," Mollie agreed. "You wouldn't believe some of the things that happened," she went on. Cindy felt Mollie was coming awfully close to blurting out her misadventures. She felt there were some things their parents would be just as well off not knowing. She was pretty sure that if Mollie thought about it for a minute, she'd feel the same way. She decided to divert her attention.

"You and I have dish duty, Mollie," Cindy said, standing up and collecting plates. Mollie joined her, and they were soon down by the creek, filling up jugs with water to wash the breakfast dishes.

"Mollie," Cindy began. "I don't think Mom and Dad need to know about everything that happened this weekend. Like forgetting to feed the cats and not bringing food for Winston."

"And about setting up the practical joke on me?"

"Yes, and about your scary canoe trip," Cindy said.

"Cindy's right, Mollie," Nicole said, joining her sisters at the edge of the creek. "We don't need to tell Mom and Dad about the cats or the canoe trip."

"All right. I guess I can keep my lips sealed about how you guys messed up my tent and stole my blueberries."

"We didn't steal your blueberries," Cindy said adamantly.

"Honest?"

"Honest," Cindy assured her. "And you're the one who left your tent in a terrible mess to begin with, not us. We only added to it a little bit."

"That's right," Nicole added. "When we went inside, it was a pigpen, just like your room always is."

"Well, I don't get it," Mollie said. "I swear it was neat when I left it."

"Are you sure?" Cindy asked.

"Of course I'm sure," Mollie assured her sisters.

"Uh-oh," Cindy said. "That can only mean one thing."

"Just one," Nicole agreed.

"Oh, no," Mollie said in disbelief. "You don't really think there was a bear at the campsite, do you?" Her sisters nodded.

"Mollie, could you show me how to make a hammock for tonight?" Nicole asked.

The image of all five of the Lewises imprisoned in hammocks slung between trees at the campsite was too much. The girls laughed helplessly while they finished washing up. When their laughter was under control, they slung their arms across each other's shoulders and marched back up to the campsite, singing "Vista Stands for Victory" at the top of their lungs.

Here's a look at what's ahead in NEVER A DULL MOMENT, the eleventh book in Fawcett's "Sisters" series for GIRLS ONLY.